JOHN MACKAY returns to his Hebridean roots for his second novel *Heartland*. His acclaimed first novel, *The Road Dance*, featured in the Scottish bestsellers list. It has been translated into Danish and is soon to be translated into German. John is the anchorman on Scottish TV's evening news programme *Scotland Today* and has reported on many of the major news stories in Scotland in recent times. He is married with two sons and lives in Renfrewshire.

By the same author:
The Road Dance, Luath Press, 2002

Heartland

JOHN MACKAY

Luath Press Limited

EDINBURGH

www.luath.co.uk

First published 2004
This edition 2005

John MacKay has asserted his rights
under the Copyright, Designs and Patents Act 1988
to be identified as the author of this work.

The paper used in this book is recyclable.
It is made from low-chlorine pulps produced in a low-
energy, low-emission manner from renewable forests.

Printed and bound by
Bookmarque Ltd, Croydon

Typeset in 10.5 point Sabon

© John MacKay, 2004

For those whose bonds are tied to No. 2

Acknowledgements

My thanks to Donnie Macintosh, all but a brother.
Sandra Riddel and Joey Darroch, ever-willing first
draft readers. Also Chrissie Macintosh, Katie Mary
Macdonald and Ina Smith. And Martin Smith the angler.

Mairi MacRitchie at the Gearranan Black House
Village and the folk at *An Comunn Eachdraidh
Charlabhaigh* for keeping the story alive.

My colleagues in the Glasgow and Edinburgh
newsrooms of Scottish TV. Also Bryan Wotherspoon,
whose heart must fall whenever I appear!

The many people who wrote with so much
encouragement following the publication of
The Road Dance. Gavin MacDougall,
Nele Andersch, Jennie Renton and all at Luath.

Above all, Joyce for her love and support
and Scott and Ross for all the joy.

Chapter One

THIS WAS HIS land. He had sprung from it and would return surely to it. Its pure air refreshed him, the big skies inspired him and the pounding seas were the rhythm of his heart. It was his touchstone. Here he renourished his soul.

The landscape was eternal, the rock smelted at the beginning of time. But the mark of man was all around. Where once there had been trees, now there was none. Science said it had been the change of climate, but he preferred to believe the legends that the Vikings of a thousand years before had scorched the earth.

Out on a promontory there was a pile of stones that in a different millennium had been the hideaway chapel of a hermit priest. A large stone slab on the moor covered the resting place of an unknown seaman from another century. Regular folds in the ground where the grass grew greenest had been the food-providing lazybeds of his forebears. Carefully constructed cairns stood on the hilltops, tributes to people lost in time. And all about, ruins of the old houses, where once there had been ceilidhs and warmth and life.

With no forests, the wind was free to roam, swooping, swirling and unceasing. Sometimes he imagined the spirits of those long gone were borne on the breezes that kept the constant company of the old stones. To the eye it was a place of emptiness, where all who mattered were gone and time had passed on. Yet on another plane it was alive, vital with forces beyond understanding.

The peat was still sodden from the spring rain, the water

gurgling through the earth beneath his feet, sometimes gathering in an oily sheen in the hollows and dips. There would be no rain today though. The ocean stretched away beyond sight, an overwhelming vastness beneath the blue, cloudless sky.

Iain Martin was at the old house, on a hill overlooking the village road as it merged into the foreshore of the bay. From this point you could see to the horizon with its allure and promise, and behind, the houses of the district haphazardly dotted along the general line of the road. It was where the unknown and the familiar came together. Among the ruins of lives long gone, the silence and isolation could be both soothing and forlorn.

The sea lapped and lolled, but he well knew how treacherous it could be. While the land was his comfort, the water scared him. How dark and awesome it could turn. For as long as man had fished, the ocean had gathered payback. Iain's generation had been no different and the memory of how his friend Rob had been lost stuck to him like a limpet.

Iain should have been on the boat with his friends, but there were books to be studied for his exam resits. Rob had strolled off with Neilie towards the sea, smiling as ever, his rubber boots flapping against each other at the knees. That sound had stayed with Iain. He wondered whether the water-filled boots dragged his friend down while the breath seeped away from his lungs. And though Neilie had cursed Iain for backing out of their planned trip and cajoled him about getting fresh air in his head, Rob had been his usual easygoing self. There were fish to be caught, beer to be drunk and life to be enjoyed. Even now, Iain could see Rob's face framed by a thick black fringe and sideburns, his dark eyes alight and a smile pulling constantly at his mouth. Living for the moment, that was Rob. And it was a consolation in the aftermath, as he searched for any fragment that might ease the loss, that Rob had truly lived each day.

The urgent voice of Iain's father had penetrated the deep of his sleep, jerking him into consciousness and a life that would never be the same again. His dreams of Catriona had been disturbed by the distant ringing of the phone. A light must have gone on and as he came out of his slumber he heard his father's monosyllabic voice. His father was never comfortable speaking on the phone, but Iain remembered him sounding particularly terse that night.

'Yes. Oh. Right away.'

Then the voice had called to him. Something was wrong at the shore and they were needed. Groggy from sleep, Iain stumbled from his bed into the cold of his room and pulled on his jeans and a T-shirt. His brother, Kenny, was slower to stir. As Iain emerged from his room his father had nodded at his clothes and said grimly, 'You'll be needing more than that.'

His mother, Mary, had stood at the door, her face lined with worry and her dressing-gown pulled tightly around her. She had been standing beside her husband throughout the short telephone call, a little irritated that he had got to it first, and anxious to hear what was wrong at that time of night.

'Someone's missing,' Iain's father had said. 'One of the boys raised the alarm at Dan's. That was Nan asking us to go down and help.'

'What boy?' asked Iain.

'She didn't know. Dan just called to her before going. C'mon, we need to be quick.'

Even then, as he pulled on an old oilskin and his boots, Iain couldn't quite believe that it might be one of his friends.

The wind barged in as soon as they opened the door. When they stepped away from the protection of the house, the rain nipped their faces hard. Iain and Kenny might be approaching their twenties, with all the confidence that brings, but at times like this they still looked to their father for leadership. They could bring youth and strength, but that would be no match for the understanding and sense that came with experience.

Dan and Nan's house sat at the final bend in the road before it twisted down to the shoreline. Nan was standing outside waiting for them.

'They're all down at the shore, but there's nothing to see. I've phoned the coastguard.'

'Right, Nan,' said their father.

'I think I should maybe stay here in case anyone phones.'

'Yes. That'd be best.'

The sea was thrashing high up on the shoreline. They could make out four figures. Two of them were pulling the boat up beyond the reach of the waves. The boys' father flicked on his torch and they all looked round. It was Rob who was missing. Dan clattered over the pebbles to meet them.

'Rob's gone. Overboard. Neilie managed to get the boat back, though I don't know how.'

Iain ran to his friend. Neilie had a small whisky bottle in his hand and he was soaked through, his hair plastered so flat that the skin of his scalp could be seen white against it. His whole body was trembling.

'Neilie, what happened?'

Neilie shook his head, unable to speak.

Iain's father came over, speaking loudly over the wind.

'You need to get up to the house and get dry.'

'No,' protested Neilie, 'we've got to get him.'

'We'll get him. But if you don't get warmed up then we'll have another problem.'

'Dan's given me a shot of this. That'll warm me.'

'Neilie,' Iain's father commanded, 'get up to the house and get warm. There's others will look for him. Iain, help him up.'

Iain hauled his friend up and led him unsteadily back up the shore, their feet slipping on the pebbles. A huddle of villagers had gathered, lashed by the rain and pulled by the wind. Clips of raised voices carried, indistinct but concerned.

'Will they find him?' Neilie asked desperately.

'They'll find him,' reassured Iain. 'I'm sure of it.'

The hours of the night had passed too quickly, taking hope with them. By morning, the storm had blown out and the sea ceased to flay the land. In the bleak light of a grey dawn all was settled, except for figures scrambling over the cliff edges looking for something, for anything, and the men in the lifeboat scanning the sea back and forth outside the bay. From wherever any of the searchers looked back, they would have seen the woman standing at the rim of the shore, a blue nylon nightdress flapping beneath a heavy anorak. Rob's mother had come as soon as she'd heard, taking time only to grab one of her son's jackets for protection. She had sunk deeper and deeper into its folds as the hours passed, refusing to abandon her watch. By the end of hope she was withdrawn into herself.

Rob's father had desperately scoured the cliffs for days and it was commonly held that his spirit died the night he knew his boy was not returning.

At Nan's house, Neilie had been dried and warmed. His own mother had rushed in, barely knowing what to do in her relief, pulling his head to her as the tears coursed down her face. Neilie's father carried on to join the search, as relieved as his wife at learning their son was safe, but unable to show it. Iain went with him, leaving Neilie in the care of the women folk.

When Iain returned later, Catriona was there, her young face drawn and pale. She was seated on the floor beside Neilie, her hand holding his as he drank tea and tried to stop shivering. When Iain came in she, like all the others in the room, could immediately tell from his face that there was no news.

'What will we do without Rob?' she had asked tearfully when she saw him to the door on his way back to rejoin the search.

The four of them, Catriona, Rob, Neilie and Iain, had been the youth of a fading community. With few alternatives for playmates, Catriona had tagged herself determinedly to them. They had resented her at first, but when she proved over time to be their equal at running, climbing and fishing she became an honorary boy with them. As they grew, she blossomed and Iain's heart was hers for the taking.

The faces of the older men were set grim. In times before, when more fishing was done from these shores, searches for people lost overboard – for entire crews – had been more frequent and so often in vain. None of those who knew of the grip of the sea carried much hope. But they tried painstakingly for one who was their own. Every cleft of cliff was examined at great risk and the boat was even set on the water again. But the silence of their returns said enough.

Neilie recovered. Physically he was in his prime, young and strong. If there were any scars on his mind he hid them well, but never in all the years since had he ever talked to Iain about the loss of their friend.

Rob's mother, widowed two years later, had endured until her death, but no more than that. The boys made a point of calling on her and she always welcomed them, but they could see the emptiness in her eyes. Her heart was burdened with thoughts of her only child, lost to the sea.

The night it happened remained clear for Iain. His memory of the subsequent investigation and inquiry was a jumble. One report recorded the good fortune and skill that allowed Neilie to pilot the boat back to shore with only one oar and raise the alarm. Neilie had become quite the local hero with his stories of the snarling sea and the jagged rocks. People marvelled at his seamanship and said it was a miracle he had got back to land at all.

Rob's body was never found, its fate not dwelt upon. How fine, Iain had pondered in darker moments, were the contours of fate, how one could be lost and another saved. What had taken Rob overboard and left Neilie to survive? What thought, step or movement had placed Rob in the hands of eternity? He had heard the same asked by the veterans of the Great War, whose time was drawing to a close during his youth. A bullet had grazed the back of his own grandfather's head, he remembered.

'I don't know why I turned,' the old man would say. 'Nobody called me, but I turned my head to the side. That's when, crack!' And he would illustrate with the tip of his finger how the bullet had clipped the skin off the back of his head.

The veterans were always reluctant to talk of those times, but sometimes they did and always they questioned why they had survived and their comrades had not. They had no answer for it.

Predestination is what the church had told them and the generations that followed. It was all part of God's design. You lived your life as God planned it for you. At the memorial service for Rob the minister had reinforced that view. It would serve no purpose for anyone, and he meant Rob's parents and Neilie himself, to agonise over why one had been taken and one spared. It was the Lord's choosing and it was not for mortal man to understand the Wisdom of His way.

His grandfather believed that to be as good an explanation as any, but it never rested easily with Iain. Why live your life at all, if that were so? And especially, why ponder the great choices of faith and life when there was no choice at all?

When he was younger, he would sometimes be dismissive of the committed faith of the old folk around him. He had been the first of his family to attend university, although Kenny came soon after and his sister Christine would follow. My, my, the university! What store his parents laid in the wisdom to be received there and the opportunities it would open.

His studies had made him disdainful of the certainties with which the previous generations had lived their lives. Now he wasn't so sure. His forebears had lived life in the raw, dependent upon the seasons and exposed to the relentless realities of a hard life. For so long in their youth, his grandfather's generation had walked daily with death and horror. What arrogance was it that made him think his learning from books was superior to theirs?

He was never sure whether Neilie was bothered with such preoccupations, despite having been so close to eternity. Probably not. 'Get up to that bar,' was his philosophy.

Nearly twenty years on, Iain was home again, watching the deceptive lap of the water. How peaceful it seemed and yet how remorseless it could be.

From his vantage point he could see the headland of the bay facing onto open sea. It was said that a baby had been thrown into the sea from there, a newborn boy. Iain had heard the story often from his mother.

'The poor child was washed up on the shore, all wrapped up. Oh, it must have been terrible. His mother couldn't have been in her right mind to do something like that.'

'Who was she?'

'No one knows. Some said she wasn't from the village, that he'd been put in the sea further up the coast, but my mother remembers them searching up on the cliffs around here. The old captain who found him told my grandmother that the child hadn't been in the water long enough to have come from somewhere else. It must have been a local girl.'

'And they never found out who?'

'Not for sure. You remember Kirsty Seanacharrach?'

'Yes, in at the shore? Died just a couple of years ago?'

'Well, and I shouldn't be saying this, but she had a sister Annie who died when she was young. She had that terrible flu after the war. Anyway, some thought it was her. They had the police over and everything, but they never did find out.'

'Why did they think it was her?'

'My granny said there had been doctors at the house at

the time, but nothing ever happened. I suppose it was just rumour.'

'What about Kirsty Seanacharrach? Did she never say anything?'

'No. She was very nice. Remember she always gave you children sweets when you were going down to the shore? She was very quiet, Kirsty, she didn't really speak much. But here's the thing, and I was only just hearing of this.' His mother became almost conspiratorial. 'The baby was buried in the cemetery. There was no headstone for the wee soul, but sometimes you'd see flowers at this spot in the graveyard. Nobody knew who placed them there, but now and again a posy would be left. Well, just recently a woman in the church was saying to me that she'd only just noticed, but since the old woman died there have been no flowers on the child's grave.'

'Really? You mean, they think old Kirsty was the child's mother?'

'Who knows? These secrets all die with the dead.'

Iain remembered that clearly now. Beneath his shaking legs lay a skeleton, exposed to the skies for the first time in how long? Another secret only the dead knew?

Chapter Two

THE DAY HAD started with a spade in his hand and peace in his soul. Now he was trembling, staring down on the exposed grave of someone unknown.

On a plateau just before the land dropped finally away to the sea, stood the roofless remains of an old blackhouse. For half a century it had been open to the wind, the rains and the storms of the ocean and still it stood, defiant and enduring. Now it seemed as elemental as the natural forces that had sought to destroy it for so long. The construction of grey gneiss rock had been hewn from the land around and the uneven stones were bound together, not by mortar, but by the intricate assembly of the skilled builder. Iain was a direct descendent of that builder.

Nature's force had not yet made it succumb: in time far distant, the land would more subtly reclaim its own. The house was overgrown inside with grass and moss and carpeted with buttercups and bluebells. A platform of turf had formed around the top of the steadfast walls.

Time had swept over the house and left it behind. Yet the changes that had encouraged its people to move on to greater comforts could now be utilised to bring it back to life. Iain would be the one to complete the circle.

It was easy to get romantic here, to absorb the glory of nature – the awesome Atlantic, the moorland flowers and the birds gliding on the wing. But that would be to ignore the gloom of winter when depression could sink a lonely soul. It would be to forget that sorrow seeped through the soil. Economic fragility had forced so many away. There were those who had left at the first opportunity, eager to escape the claustrophobia of everyone knowing who you were and who your people were.

Adventure, education and opportunity had all been reasons for leaving, but more than anything it had been love. Lost love. Iain had fled from having to face that love every day, knowing that it could not be fulfilled.

Now he was home again, home for good. There was no denying the bonds of blood and soil. He had always known the island would be his home again, that he would return to the very land that his family had abandoned two generations before.

'Why would you want to do that?' his mother, Mary, had asked, taken aback. 'You'd be better to build yourself something new, if that's what you want to do. The old place is best left alone.'

'I thought you would understand, Mam. You of all people.'

'Well, I don't. I can't see that it makes sense. No one has lived there in sixty years. And they had good reason to leave. Why would you want to live in it now, even if you could?'

Neilie was more to the point.

'You're pissed!'

Iain smiled when he remembered the conversation in the hotel bar.

'The only people who come up with daft ideas like that are those from the south who have more money than sense,' had been Neilie's firm opinion. 'They come here and try to change everything and then when they realise it's not the good life, they'll bugger off back to where they came from. But you? Bloody hell! You'll forget about it in the morning.'

'Why not?'

'Why not? Loads of reasons, but here's two for starters. Your old lady has a house with a roof and windows for when you come home. Second of all, the place is a ruin and you aren't a builder. Now stop talking crap and get up to that bar.'

They would come round in time. It wasn't the good life he wanted. He had been born and raised on the island and he knew that it was no idyll. What he wanted, what he really needed, was peace. Everything he had done since, his career, his marriage, his whole lifestyle had been an attempt to fulfil ambitions that he had absorbed from other people, not what was truly his own. He was done with running and he was home.

Neilie was right. He wasn't a builder and he didn't know where to begin, but stripping the house down to its basic structure and then reconstructing it, you didn't need to be an analyst to see the therapy in that. The essentials of his life were here. This is where he could be himself. He knew that now.

The ceremonial cutting of the first sod the previous day hadn't worked out quite as he had imagined. The spade couldn't cut cleanly through the soil because of the tangle of grass and roots. It barely penetrated any earth at all: first evidence that it would be a long slog ahead.

Iain had cautioned himself against getting too carried away with his project. He was highly aware of the symbolism of cutting the first turf. He would not work so hard the first day, just make a start. Then he would bring the barrow down and make real progress. He had toasted his life ahead with a slug of whisky from a hip flask before grabbing the spade. The whisky was still on his tongue when the jarring from the spade rattled up his spine. The rewards of living in such a landscape were glorious, but nothing had ever been won from it without backbreaking graft.

He took a breath and jumped heavily onto the spade. Then again and again. Finally it severed through the grass and weeds and he felt the blade sink beneath him. Sweat smeared his forehead and his lungs dilated.

This was his first challenge. He could stop now, walk away and laugh at his foolishness. Or he could thrust his spade down again. The motivation in ages past would have been dig or starve. Iain was spared that. His choice was between reason and pride, realism and dream. He stepped back, grasped the hip flask from his backpack and took another swig of the uisge beatha, the water of life, then wiped his forearm against his head. Lifting the spade up, he drove it down, lunging from his shoulder.

That same shoulder ached four hours later as he soaked in a bath drawn by his mother. Not just his shoulder, but his neck, his back and his thighs. This was exhaustion like he had not experienced in many a year. In his former, office-bound existence, the fatigue of routine and long hours had never matched this. As a young man back from the peat cutting, the prospect of a few beers at the hotel had been enough to reinvigorate his youthful body. With middle-age not so far ahead now, it would take longer to recover, but he reassured himself that his muscles would become used to the effort.

Despite the aching and the nipping of the blisters on his palms, he had a feeling of achievement, satisfaction in a hard job well done. He had worked out a technique and had been shifting far more turf by the end of the day than at the beginning.

On day two he had uncovered the remains of the original clay and stone floor of the house. Perhaps he might find where the old open fire had been, the focal point of the house. At the beginning of the century, when the family was getting a little more prosperous, a chimney stack had been built at the top end. No more smoke swirling around the interior all day, wisping through the small hole in the roof and blackening the thatch. What a step forward that must have been! A peat fire would burn again in that hearth, but Iain liked his comforts and so electricity would fire his central heating too. For that, the old floor would have to go.

The blisters still bothered him, but the ache in his muscles receded more quickly now and his stamina was improving. Developing a steady rhythm he had removed most of the turf and had used the barrow to pile it outside. It was remarkable how absorbed he could become. The time would fly. Sometimes he missed the breaks he had set for himself, but then he could sit with his sandwiches, made from black-crusted bread, and his whisky, and feel that real progress had been made.

Already the house seemed familiar, the contours of the stones and the patterns of lichen on them. The construction was so different from the straight, geometric lines of bricks and cement. The big stones were the key, some of them too big for one man to lift alone. None was a regular shape, the edges weren't straight and the corners ranged through all the angles from acute to obtuse. Smaller stones were packed into the gaps and from this complex jumble emerged a sturdy structure which was a work of art in its own way. It took a craftsman to see how this clutter of forms and shapes could be fused together to create something so lasting.

When he had finished, the floor of what had been the original living area of the house was cleared. An additional room had been built on the seaward side and that would be next. At the far end there was an opening into a smaller space which would have been the animal byre.

Iain stood with his back to the chimney stack and surveyed his work. This was the very floor that had been the hearth of his forefathers, the surface on which they had walked, cooked, talked and lived their lives. What joys and sorrows had these walls witnessed? More than one hundred and fifty years of one family's history. Birth and death, joy and loss. The cries of newborns and the final sighs of the dying. It was all around him. He could feel it. It was part of who he was. They lived on through him.

How often had his great-grandmother swept this floor? In the one faded photograph his family had of her, her face was weather-beaten, her hair scraped back in a severe middle parting, her dress black and her gaze solemn and steady. She had been born only yards from here, had never left the island, and in this house she had passed on to eternity. The village had been her world. When she died, the house had been closed up.

By day three he was ready to break through what remained of the clay floor, wielding a pickaxe to get going. Everything had been built to last, in an expectation of endurance alien to the mindset of Iain's generation, by people who had suffered clearances and uncertainty of tenure. Finally, the family secured land they could call their own. This house was testament to that faith, solid and enduring. Here, where the Atlantic made landfall from its restless journeying, they had torn rock from the ground, borne boulders from the shore, and built a home. Fish bountiful in the sea, crops in the ground, family and faith. For a few, too few golden years, that is how it was.

Politics, economics and war had changed it all, and then changed it again and again. But the house was a memorial to his great-grandfather's belief that he had found his heartland. Iain's heart told him the same.

The core of the house would remain, but much would have to change. It was easier once he had made the initial penetration of the clay. That gave him leverage and he worked at it, using the pick to break it up and then scooping up the fragments with the shovel and dumping it in the barrow. He would keep the rubble and reuse it once he had dug further down.

Swinging the pickaxe pulled on different muscles from the digging and he had to take frequent rests. Sitting on top of the wall, he looked down on the little bay below him. It was more like the imprint of an index finger than a sweeping cove. All down the coastline there were inlets and bays like this, where the ocean had probed for weakness in the land. Barely two miles south-west of here, it had penetrated, carving a sea loch deep into the core of the island. Its name, like so many on the island, came from the Vikings of the Norwegian fiords. Masters of the sea, they had understood its importance for shelter and settlement. As had others before them, peoples lost in the mists of history. Their Neolithic structures of worship were beyond modern understanding, but it was clear what would have drawn them here: protection from the howl of the merciless Atlantic. That recognition linked Iain's people to prehistoric man.

Beyond the sealoch, on its far shores, he could see the ocean break onto deserted golden sands. A flock of seabirds circled and soared around the scatter of large rocks that stood as defiant islets against the spread of the sea. The same scenes had played before the eyes of ages.

In the mid-nineteenth century when this house was first built, there would have been small boats on the shingle, beyond the tug of the tide. Ships of crafted wood and billowing sail would have been sighted out beyond the inshore currents. If his imagination ran deep, Iain could see his great-grandmother spinning at the doorway and her husband repairing fishing nets spread over the fence. The scene before him had such a timeless quality, yet only fifty yards up the road the modern world made its bold mark through the television aerials and steel cars.

Iain climbed down off the wall and resumed his task. Pebbles brought from the shore formed the hardcore of the floor. It would all have to come out. He had started breaking through at the gable end. From there, the floor sloped gently downwards, giving him a relatively flat surface over which to roll his barrow. Livestock would have been kept in the byre at the bottom end of the house and the slope was intended to ensure that their waste ran away from the living quarters.

On the wall at right angles to the gable end, near to the chimney, there was a cavity that would once have held a small wooden box containing his great-grandfather's Bible and spectacles. Iain had begun digging where his chair would have been and where, nightly, he would have read from the Good Book. The old man's wife would have sat opposite him.

As Iain worked his way across the opening of the fireplace, the sun began to sink towards the horizon. In gathering shadow, he deposited a last scoop of rubble into the barrow. It had been a long day, but a satisfying one. Leaning on the spade, he looked over the wall towards the setting sun. Then, as he turned to throw the spade on top of the barrow, something caught his eye. A fragment of cloth. His curiosity roused, he tugged at it, but couldn't release it any further. It was stuck fast in the earth. Discoloured and dirt-stained, the cloth appeared to be plain, without pattern or embroidery. More than likely it was nothing significant, but Iain knew that it would scratch at his mind through the night if he left it now. It shouldn't take too long to free. He dug away a bit more, pulled at the cloth and then dug again.

He couldn't imagine anything of value being buried here; it was unlikely even to be of interest. But Iain was so involved in the house now, that his imagination was constantly encouraged to life.

Soon, the sun had gone completely and the gloomy half-light of dusk was creeping around him. He scraped away at the clay, exposing more of the cloth as he worked. Some rocks appeared to have been used to weigh it down and he began to sense that it really was something significant.

More than an hour had passed by the time he had exposed the entire length of the sheet. Parts of it had rotted away and he had inadvertently torn it in places, but he still couldn't make out what was beneath. All he could tell was that parts of the bundle seemed to be long and hard.

He was excited. Could it be weapons of some sort? Weapons, rifles and swords, had been hidden in the thatch of the houses in the wake of the 1745 Rebellion, but that was long before the foundations of this house had been laid. Perhaps it might be guns brought home from the Napoleonic wars, or the Indian Wars of the American

Prairies, or even souvenirs from Flanders trenches. Men from this village had fought in them all.

If his guess was right, there might be something of value here.

He lifted off one of the rocks at the end of the sheet and slowly peeled back the top layer. Clumps of dirt clung to it, adding to its weight. Nothing was revealed but more sheeting, which had been rolled over and over a number of times. He would either have to lift it out and unravel it all, or cut through it.

He remembered there was a combination knife in the car. The exhaustion in his muscles made him think about leaving it until the morning, but curiosity pushed him on.

As the village road meandered down towards the shoreline, the tar surface gave way to an overgrown, stony track just as it began the final incline, about a hundred yards from the foreshore. Iain had parked his car at the end of the surfaced road because he always enjoyed walking down that last stretch, watching the bay spread out gradually before him.

Suddenly, he heard a roaring engine and then almost instantly a car, with headlights full on, came racing round the final bend in the road and skidded to a halt.

Neilie's head thrust out of the window.

'Have you had enough?' he shouted. 'I didn't even know you'd started.'

'Nearly finished,' smiled Iain.

'You're working too hard, cove. Leave it. I'll come down with the digger and do the hard work. Anyway, Catriona wants you to come up for your dinner. She left a message with your mother, but you've not been back all day. I thought you were having a holiday before you started this. You should have been up at our place by now. Get yourself a shower and we'll see you when you're ready.'

With that, he gunned the engine, the tyres spat stones, and he was away. Typical Neilie. When an idea took him he was all busy and wasn't receptive to discussion. Iain hadn't even been able to tell him about his find. Still, Iain was determined enough in his own way and he would find out what was wrapped in the sheeting before he did anything else.

As he walked back with the knife, he thought of seeing Catriona again, this time without the shelter of his own marriage for protection. She was the girl who'd broken his heart all those years before by choosing someone else. Not just anyone, but his best friend. It was one of many confrontations he would have to make if this new life was to be truly a fresh beginning.

He cursed himself for not having brought a torch, but he hadn't expected to be working into the darkness. He was his own boss, after all.

Kneeling over the hole, he stretched a section of the sheet taut and thrust the blade into it. It wasn't a straightforward process and he had to get down into the hollow and hack continually at the material, revealing another layer, and another. Sweat trickled down his temples and the back of his neck.

Finally, he cut through a layer and found nothing underneath. Using both hands, he pulled at the opening in the material, widening the tear, trying to control the urge to yank indiscriminately in case he damaged what lay beneath.

Suddenly, without any dawning realisation, he saw a ribcage, unmistakable even to a layman's eye. Iain instinctively recoiled, then with a deep breath, he looked back down. Beneath the rip in the cloth he could plainly see three pairs of ribs curling away from a central point, the unseen breastbone. They were not the clean white bone that matched his mind's image, but bones they were, stained and yellowed, with fragments of unknown substances attached to them.

Iain stepped back out of the hole trying to comprehend what he was seeing.

'It might be nothing,' he thought. The last word was uttered aloud. A rush of questions coursed through his mind. What was it? Was it human? Why was it here?

He went to his knapsack and took out a packet of cigarettes, then pulled himself up onto the top of the wall and sat there smoking, looking down into the hole.

If it was an animal, by the size of the bones it must have been a big one. Livestock were a familiar part of growing up in a crofting community. Iain had helped his father with the sheep and they had had a dairy cow. These bones were too big to have come from a sheep or a dog, and too small for a cow.

He must expose the entire skeleton to be certain. Jumping off the wall, he resumed digging. It didn't take long.

When he found the skull, there was no doubt. It was human, without any question. A grotesque image familiar from horror films and comic book stories. The teeth transfixed him. There was something very personal about teeth. When this person had smiled or talked, these teeth would have been visible to others. Two were missing, one from the front of the bottom jaw and an incisor from just above.

Iain stood up again and sat back on top of the wall, taking a swig of whisky from his flask. He lit another cigarette, inhaling deeply, and tried to make some sense of what he had discovered.

This was someone's burial place. It couldn't be an archaeological discovery, because it would have been uncovered when the house was constructed. This person had been buried since the house was built. Had they been laid there when the house was still occupied, or had they been buried in the years since it was empty? It was sinister, either way.

The breeze coming in off the sea seemed to rise and ruffle his hair. The grass and rushes bowed a little more and he heard a wave fall onto the shore. In his heightened state, he sensed restlessness around him.

Chapter Three

THE PALE GLOW of the shroud was soon all that Iain could see in the darkness. He would have to leave everything and return the following day. He might not sleep soundly this coming night, but it was unlikely he would have done anyway. In the daylight he would be more composed and less likely to miss something.

He pulled the torn sheet together as best he could and weighted it with stones, uncomfortably conscious that he was placing the rocks on someone's body. He reassured himself that this was the best he could do to protect the remains.

The chill of the falling night wriggled through his clothes as he walked slowly back up to his car. As soon as he started the engine and flipped on the headlights, he felt connected with the present again. As he drove along the road, an almost supernatural flash of glowing green eyes startled him, although he knew already that it was only a sheep caught in his beams. All else was dark and foreboding.

It took barely a minute to drive to his mother's. The outside light was on and the warm, inviting glow from the kitchen spilled out as he pulled off the road. He felt strangely like a child coming home after being lost in the dark.

She came to the door.

'There you are! Goodness, you've been there all day. That's too much for anyone. Now, I haven't made you any dinner because Catriona and Neilie want you to go round there.'

His mother's chatter calmed his nerves.

'You look wabbit,' she said sympathetically. 'Take a seat, a' ghraidh.' When he was a child she had only used that term of endearment when she was consoling him. She had used it a lot since he'd come home.

'No, I'll need to have a bath.' He groaned involuntarily as he moved his throbbing frame towards the bathroom.

'Would you not be better staying at home? You look fit for your bed.'

'No, Neilie's decided, and you know what he's like. There'll be trouble if I don't go.'

He hobbled through to the living-room from the kitchen, leaning on door handles until his legs got going again.

'Look at you,' his mother laughed. 'This'll be the death of you. I'll have a cup of tea ready when you get out. And before I forget, Yvonne called.'

'What did she want?'

'She didn't say. I told her you were out.'

'Was that all?'

'What else is there to say, a' ghraidh?'

'She didn't say why she was calling?'

'Yvonne was never one to tell me much. You know that.'

There was no denying it. Yvonne and his mother had always had an uneasy relationship. There had never been unpleasantness, but they hadn't connected. Yvonne was not what Mary had expected for her son's wife and Yvonne could not get in tune with her mother-in-law. Perhaps Mary had always known that she was not the one for him.

Life with Yvonne hadn't been unhappy, it had just not been fulfilling. There had been laughter, genuine fondness and no shortage of warm recollections, but they had come to realise that there was no love. Iain had hoped that

Yvonne would be the one who would exorcise Catriona from his heart and for a spell he believed that to be so. But in time he knew he was wrong, and although he tried never to betray it, Yvonne knew. She had told him that this was not love as she had hoped it would be, that he had to give something back. That he couldn't was confirmation that they had no future together. During a long night of truths and tears, they agreed to let each other go. Never had he felt so badly about himself as a human being. His betrayal of Yvonne's hopes scarred his view of himself.

These last few months had been life-changing. The company was making cutbacks and redundancy packages were available. Iain's job was to be relocated to London, or he could take the money – and his chances.

He would not have had the courage to make such a drastic move on his own, but with the decisions on his marriage and his career being made by others, he had come home, to where he wanted to be.

'Don't forget to phone Yvonne,' Mary said after he'd changed. 'I'll bring your tea to you.'

Iain went through to the phone in the living room. The peat fire in the grate was down to a glow. He sat on the old settee facing it. On one side of the fire was his mother's seat with its magazine rack and knitting bag, on the other side was the chair that had been his father's. The impression of his outline remained and Iain had never felt comfortable using it. How often in the city he'd thought of her sitting there on a winter's night, alone with his father's chair. Only once had he tried to persuade her to get a new suite, but she wouldn't hear of it.

Yvonne was living at her parents and he shifted uncomfortably as he heard the repeating tones before she answered. How could he be nervous speaking to the woman with whom he'd shared so much?

'Hello?'

'Hi, it's me.'

'Hi. Thanks for phoning.'

'Thanks for phoning!' he thought. How formal was that? Is this what they were reduced to? Talking in formalities, observing the protocols of strangers?

'How are you?' Iain heard himself asking.

'Fine. Fine. You know that job I applied for?'

There had been little he had known about his wife in those final months. She had been intent on setting up her new life and since he wasn't going to be part of it, there was no reason to involve him in her plans. Her friends had given her all the counselling and advice she needed.

'The job I went for in London? You don't remember, do you? Well, anyway, I got it.'

Her voice didn't convey celebration, just information. There was a momentary silence as he tried to form a suitable response. No hugging her and kissing her and spinning her round in his arms. No celebratory drinks or dinner. Iain didn't know what to say.

'I'm going. At the end of next week.'

'Oh,' was all that Iain could manage.

'It's just that we've had an offer for the house and there's papers I need to get you to sign. And you still haven't moved your stuff out.'

'I didn't realise there was a rush.'

'Iain, you know we're trying to sell the house. It doesn't help with all your things lying around. Anyway, there's no point in going over old ground. Can you make it down early next week and we can get this sorted before I leave?'

'Yeah, I should be able to do that.'

He could see her now. A new hairstyle, a well-cut suit

that flattered, but hardened her. The make-up would be subtle, but plentiful. Yvonne was shedding her old persona and the ties that went with it.

'I'll call you.'

'Yeah.' He paused, wanting to say something else. 'Okay. Bye.'

Iain sat for a while, surprised by his reaction to her news. He realised he was missing her and would have liked to have been there with her. She was still his wife and here, apart from her, it was easy to forget the antagonism that had sparked between them so often. He could hardly complain that she was moving on. She had no idea of his plans to settle back on the island. He had wanted to avoid her scorn, caring enough about what she thought. Yvonne had no regard for his opinions now. She was leaving him behind and it was an afterthought to let him know. It hurt and he didn't really understand why.

His mother brought him a cup of tea and he drank it in silence. There was much to think about.

His sombre mood lifted when he saw Catriona. After all the years, she still warmed his blood. Her mass of dark hair had been cut gradually shorter as she got older, but it had lost none of its movement and harmony. Soft lines spread from her deep blue eyes now and her prominent, rounded cheekbones had lost the ruddiness of youth. With that maturity came an added allure. She was more lovely now than ever. What Catriona had, exuded from deep within and was much more than the surface veneer of beauty.

He constantly had to check himself from gazing at her, drawn by the life in her eyes and the turn of her mouth when she smiled. In every way, physically, emotionally, even chemically it seemed, she was the one. Always the one. And it tore at him anew that she had borne another man's children, lived in his home and shared his bed. All the worse that the man was his oldest friend.

They had all grown up together, played, cried and danced through their formative years. There were so many rites of passage he had shared with Neilie. And with Rob. Never forgetting Rob. They had coughed over the first cigarette together – a roll-up made from tobacco and a Rizla paper pinched from Neilie's father. The three of them had hidden in the loft of the barn on Iain's croft, he and Rob impatiently urging Neilie to roll the cigarette quicker as he laboured, trying vainly to copy his father's casual technique. One of the discarded matches used in the initial attempts to light the loosely packed cigarette had nearly sent the barn up in smoke.

They had got drunk for the first time together, hiding in the old house. How quickly they had begun giggling over the bottle of Woodpecker cider and three cans of beer that Neilie had pilfered during a Hogmanay party. Catriona had found them that night. She'd liked the sweetness of the cider, but the bitterness of the beer had made her screw up her face. They'd laughed at her and glugged from the cans in a manly manner, but were happy for her to remain.

For a couple of years, a Saturday night of surreptitious drinking could be the highlight of any month. One of the older boys could always be persuaded to buy them some cans, receiving one himself in payment. Then they would go back to saving hard for the next session.

It was Catriona who first suggested they should all go to the dancing. She was maturing faster than they were, no longer the tomboy. She wanted other experiences, but she cared enough about them to drag them along.

The chance of getting drink was what persuaded them; it was worth the risk of being ejected for being underage. Dancing was only a dare at first, but before long the success of an evening was dictated by whether they had got off with a girl. If one of them appeared to be making progress, pulled close by a girl to rest her cheek against his, the other two would gesture unflatteringly about her looks.

Rob's easy charm made him a favourite. Neilie, physical and loud, could intimidate the girls, while Iain's studiousness did not project him as the enigma he liked to imagine himself to be. Catriona was the first girl he had ever kissed, but only because it was Catriona and she didn't count as a girlfriend. Their teeth had clattered together, he remembered that yet. He couldn't recall the first stirrings of real passion. Maybe it was seeing her long, brown legs as she swam in the sea, or perhaps one day her laugh just captivated him. What he did understand now was that by the time she had swelled to womanhood his heart was lost to her. It explained his dismay whenever she confided to him about a new boyfriend and the satisfaction he felt when it ended.

They had been together for a brief spell. How often since had his heart dragged him back to that final hot summer, when Catriona was his. But those blissful days were not as never-ending as they felt. He was going to the university and did not expect the island to be his home ever again. The city would have stifled Catriona. They both recognised their dilemma and very maturely agreed that they were young yet. Time would provide a solution. So they parted as lovers, in name at least.

During that first year when he was away, Catriona's father had died suddenly and for the one time in her life she found herself adrift, struggling for security and protection. Neilie had provided a caring embrace. That was when he realised his own unacknow- ledged love for her. He became her refuge.

When Iain returned the following summer he had kept his distance, fearful of the limits commitment would impose on his ambitions. Catriona felt he was leaving her behind and didn't want to impose. Rob's death reinforced her feelings of helplessness and loneliness and Iain did nothing to fill the void.

She found purpose in guiding Neilie back from his devastation at the loss of his friend and his gratitude overwhelmed her. He announced their engagement that New Year, to widespread astonishment. A whirlwind was how Neilie described it. Neilie had never been one for contemplation. That Iain could understand, but Cat's acceptance bewildered him. It was all so long ago, and yet his sense of the rejection remained bitterly vivid.

Iain had been the best man on their wedding day, the loneliest day of his life, watching Catriona glide enchantingly down the aisle towards Neilie and yearning so strongly to be in his place.

As the midsummer sun began to fall from the sky Iain had left the ceilidh to stand alone in the hotel gardens, jacket off, waistcoat and collar open, his kilt swinging as he walked. The lilt of the accordion band danced through the air with the laughter and whooping of the revellers inside.

Catriona had come out in her wedding gown, stunning in the soft, fading light, her face lightly flushed from the dancing. It was only when she spoke that he realised she was almost beside him.

'What brings you out here, Iain Martin? There's drink

and women inside.'

He'd grunted a laugh and mumbled about needing to cool down. She stood beside him and took his arm affectionately as they looked at the fading sun.

'I'm sure Rob is with us,' she'd said quietly. 'He wouldn't have missed this.'

She'd misunderstood his reflective mood and gripped his arm, trying to comfort them both. After some moments, he couldn't recall how long, she'd looked up and the hurt in his eyes betrayed him.

'Oh, Iain!' she'd said sadly, slipping her arms round his waist and settling her head on his chest. He'd remained stock still, resisting any impulse to touch her because it would change everything forever.

'Hey folks, is the party out here?' Neilie shouted good-humouredly, jumping onto Iain's back. The moment was gone for good.

'You're looking grim, cove. Somebody pinch the bridesmaid ahead of you?'

'Something like that,' mumbled Iain.

'We were just thinking of Rob for a moment,' said Catriona.

'Aye, well' sighed Neilie. 'I'm sure he'd have been up at the bar instead of out here. C'mon.'

They had returned to the party and danced and drank until late. Iain left before the last waltz, more drunk than he ever would be again.

It had been a long time ago. Time and their lives had moved on. They were onto the wine by the time they exhausted the local gossip.

'Of course, you're the big story yourself,' Catriona said, looking at him over her glass.

'Well, there's no doubting that,' replied Iain, swirling the Beaujolais in his glass. 'They'll be calling me all the fools of the day.'

'No,' said Catriona reflectively. 'I think most folk just think it's too much to do on your own.'

'It'll do me no harm to be on my own.'

'Oh, Iain, don't say that.'

'It's true. I'm not looking for sympathy. It'll be good for me to be on my own for a while. I don't know how long it'll last, but I'm not feeling sorry for myself. I'm doing what I want to do. That part of my life is over.'

Neilie came back from the kitchen with a glass of whisky and ice, but Catriona was focused on Iain.

'Come on,' she said sympathetically. 'You don't mean that. You and Yvonne were happy together for a long time. And who knows, maybe you can be again.'

'No chance of that. Yvonne is away and she's not coming back. Don't feel sorry for me, Cat. I don't want to get too California about it, but maybe it's a reawakening. Maybe I had to go through all that career stuff. My old man was always on about getting an education, getting a good job. Well, I did all that, and I'm not sure it was worth it. Would it have made any difference if I'd stayed here and just worked the croft or something?'

'Of course it would,' she scolded him.

'This is all too bloody serious. Just have a drink,' threw in Neilie, raising his glass.

'Neilie!' Catriona sparked at him, before turning back to Iain. 'Your father was right.'

'I don't know that he was, although he certainly believed it. Slogging away at school, slogging through university, slogging away at work. And what difference did any of it make?'

'Better than slogging away on a building site, I'll tell you that for nothing,' said Neilie, gulping a mouthful of whisky. 'I've heard all this crap before. A steady job, money in your pocket and still paid when you take a day off. Clover, boy, that's what it is, clover.'

'It doesn't feel like it, Neilie. I look back on the last twenty years and what's there to show for it? A broken marriage and a career that didn't contribute much to anything. At least what I'm doing with the old house really means something to me.'

Catriona was looking closely at him.

'Don't look at me as if I need sympathy. I don't.'

'Too right you don't,' said Neilie. 'And anyway I'll be down with the digger tomorrow and you can have the day off.'

'Honestly, I'd rather do it myself.'

Later, as they sat in the easy chairs after Neilie had drunk himself to sleep, Catriona talked more intimately.

'Are you missing her?'

'I must be. I feel very empty.'

'That's only natural.'

'Maybe, but I didn't expect to. When I played this out in my mind, I always thought of it as being free.'

'Oh we can all think like that.' She nodded at her slumbering husband with a smile.

'But it's not how it is,' Iain said regretfully, with tears glistening in his eyes. 'I keep thinking of some of the times we had.'

'And you might have again,' Catriona said encouragingly. She had moved from her chair and was sitting on the floor at his feet, her hand caressing his.

'No. Yvonne's gone. She knows the truth. I feel bad about it.'

'What d'you mean, the truth?'

'You know what the truth is.' The drink and Catriona's closeness were encouraging him to talk. 'My heart was never in it. She tried, but she lost interest. So that's why my wife is starting a new life in London and I'm sitting here pouring my heart out to you.'

Catriona stroked his hand again.

'It might have been different. But Neilie was here and I was away with my books.'

Iain had said enough.

The two of them sat watching the burning peats for a few moments. The seat of the fire glowed white-orange, and blue smoke curled up into the dark of the chimney.

'How's he doing himself?' Iain asked eventually, nodding at Neilie.

'He's just Neilie, y'know. He's been drinking more than he should,' Catriona sighed. 'He was really bad when Rob's mother died last year.'

'She didn't say anything to him, did she? She always said she didn't blame him.'

'No. I think it just brought it back to him. And she always looked so sad. She tried, but you could see it. She told my mother once that she would like him to have been buried with them.'

'After all these years? She still hoped they'd find him?'

'That's why his father stopped with the lobster pots. He was scared what he might bring up.'

'I'd heard that. It makes you think what they went through. It was bad enough for us, but I suppose we could escape it.'

Catriona was looking at Neilie.

'I don't think he's ever escaped. And it seems to be bothering him more now.'

'I could never tell how he felt. He never speaks about it?'

'He'll talk about Rob, you've heard him yourself, but not about what happened.'

'Can't blame him,' said Iain reflectively. 'You'd want to block out something like that. In all these years he's never said much, even when he's had a drink.'

'I'm worried it's the drink he's using to block it out. Look at him. When have you ever seen him fall asleep before when you've been here? And it's not even a sleep. He's had most of that bottle to himself.'

The outside door slammed and heavy footsteps could be heard in the hall.

'Is that you?' Catriona called, lifting herself onto her haunches.

A grunt of acknowledgement indicated that her sons were home. She got up and left the room and Iain could hear the teenagers' vague responses to Catriona's questions about where they'd been and what they'd been doing. He could have listened to more if he'd wanted, but soon he was lost in meditation, gazing at the fire.

By the time she returned, he was ready to go. She walked outside with him into the cool night air. There wasn't a patch of the black night sky that wasn't pierced by a star and yet all was dark.

'You're okay for going in the road?' Catriona asked him.

'I've not had much,' smiled Iain thinly.

She gripped his hand.

'Leave the regrets behind, Iain. Make this a new beginning.'

Chapter Four

'I'VE BEEN SPEAKING to Calum.'

'Calum?'

'Uncle Calum in America.'

His mother was still up when he got home.

'He was so interested in what you're doing,' she said excitedly. 'He kept talking about the 'old place'. And he was sounding so well. He just kept asking about the house. It's such a long time since he saw it last, but he could remember so much about it.'

'Did he sound annoyed?'

'Oh no, no. I told him you wanted to speak to him and he was very keen that you should. It's probably not too late to call him. It's only early evening where he is.'

'How long's he been over there?' asked Iain.

'Oh, more than sixty years now. He went over on the *Metagama* with Finlay, his brother.'

'And he's never been back?' Iain sat down at the table.

Mary shook her head.

'I've never heard much about Finlay.'

'Oh, Finlay died young. TB I think. It killed so many. I don't think they'd been away long when it happened.'

'It must have been hard for your gran.'

His mother sat down on a chair by the stove, her hands clutching a tea towel on her lap. He had seen her do this so often when she was getting involved in a conversation, distracted from what she had been doing.

'It was, it was,' she said with a wistful breathlessness.

'She never spoke about it. I suppose she would have known she would never see them again. That's how it usually was. People left for America and Canada and that was that. They were gone for good. It's different now, with the phone and the planes. Back then, all you had was the letters.'

'Who was all in the family again?'

'There were four boys and two girls. The oldest boy was lost at sea during the war. He was called Iain, like yourself. Then two girls, my own mother and Murdina. Alasdair and Finlay came after that, and then Calum was the youngest.'

'I remember Murdina's funeral. That was a couple of years ago, wasn't it?'

'My, how it poured that day. Calum is the only one left. He's into his eighties now. He was born, let me think, in 1906. So what does that make him, eighty or eighty-one?'

'And it was just the chance of work that made him leave?'

'Well there was nothing for them here,' said Mary sadly. 'They'd come through the war and there was no work, no land. And you could get... what did they call it?'

She closed her eyes as she tried to remember.

'Assisted passage?' suggested Iain. He already knew much of what she was telling him, but he liked to hear it again and again. That was how the old tales had been handed down, how they held their thrall. A story passed on by word of mouth through the generations held far more resonance than any printed record.

'That was it,' responded his mother eagerly. 'Some of them had jobs to go to as soon as they arrived. I think it was Toronto where Uncle Calum arrived. But he went to the States soon after that. He was in Duluth for a long time. At the motor factories.'

'Strange he never came home even once.'

'Well, it wasn't so easy. Calum was always interested in what was going on, but he had his family to look after. Although, in saying that, he wasn't much of a writer, not as he got older, anyway. I think I may have some of his letters somewhere. We heard a lot more from him when the phones became better.'

'I don't think I've ever spoken to him.'

'Oh, he's so nice,' said his mother warmly. 'He always asks how the family is getting on. My mother used to say he was the gentle one.'

'And he's with his daughter now?'

'Yes. Beth. He's got a room in her house.'

Their conversation began to wander off into the events of the evening and the news from Catriona and Neilie. Iain made the decision not to mention his discovery until he knew more himself. All through the chat with his mother, it had been there, a luminous mystery in his mind. What could it mean?

Since he'd started working on the house, Iain had been in his bed before midnight every night, but tonight his mind was too active. He found his great uncle Calum's number in his mother's neatly detailed address book and dialled it carefully. After a moment he heard the burr of the phone ringing across the Atlantic.

'Hello?'

The voice was deep, rasping deep, and clearly American.

'Hello. Calum?'

Iain could hear his own voice echo at the other end.

'Yes?' The voice was hesitant.

'It's Iain, Mary's son. On Lewis. She was speaking to you earlier.'

'Oh,' the voice said in friendly recognition. 'How are you, fella?'

'It's nice to speak to you at last.' Iain smiled as he spoke.

'Sure. It's taken us a while.' There was lightness in the voice now.

'I hear you're working at the old place,' said Calum.

'Yes,' answered Iain. He had known the question would come. 'I hope you don't mind.'

There was a pause. Iain wasn't sure whether it was the delay on the line, or whether the old man at the other end was thinking about it.

'No, I don't mind. I can't see what you're gonna do with it, but I don't mind at all. There can't be much left of it now.'

'You'd be surprised. The walls are still solid... well, mostly.'

'Sure. They built them to last in the old days. What you planning to do?'

'I want to live in it.'

'Good luck to you, fella. You gotta lot of work ahead. It's what, sixty years and more since it was closed up.'

'I think it'll be worth it. It's so beautiful down there at the shore.'

'We had a lot of good times there. Sad times too, mind, but mostly good. I'm the last one left. The TB got my folks. It got a lot of people round that time, the TB. They figured that the air was so pure that our lungs had no resistance. I don't know how true that is, but that's what they said.'

Uncle Calum's accent began to drift as he spoke. It was still predominantly American, but at times, on certain words, the island accent of his youth flickered through.

'That's what your brother Finlay died from too, wasn't it?' asked Iain.

'What? TB?'

'Yes.'

'Life wasn't so good to him.' It sounded like the old man was sighing.

'Why was that?'

'Ah, just he had it harder than the rest of us. The war and the tragedy and all.'

'What tragedy?'

'What was that?'

'Tragedy. You said there had been a tragedy.'

'Ah, you'll know about that son. The *Iolaire*.'

The *Iolaire*. It's all that needed to be said. The very name had haunted Lewis for generations, as embedded in the island's psyche as the names of its districts and villages. The *Iolaire*'s sinking was a catastrophe beyond comprehension that almost broke the spirit of an island that had already lost and endured so much through the Great War. Two hundred and five had died on the rocks of home. It was New Year's morning 1919 and the lights of Stornoway beckoned. A tragic misjudgement by the crew took the *Iolaire* onto the Beasts of Holm, rocks just yards from shore. On a summer's evening children could swim out to them. But in a rushing sea they were unforgiving. Most of those aboard never even made it to the decks. A few, heroes to others, just lucky to themselves, made it to the shore.

In the villages across the island, tables were laid ready for the celebrations to welcome back the men they had sent away as boys. When the door finally knocked, it was not the face they were hoping to see.

It was an unbearable irony that so many had endured the Great War only to perish within sight of home. The *Iolaire*. All that needed to be said.

'I didn't know Finlay was on the *Iolaire*,' said Iain in surprise.

'He was. Lucky to get off it too. He was one of the few,' explained Calum. 'It sure hit him hard. He lost a lot of friends. A lot of friends. Never really got over it. Changed him. He was never the same.'

Iain could hear him sigh again at the other end of the line.

'Poor Finlay,' repeated Calum.

Iain steered the conversation in a different direction.

'When was the house closed up?'

He had to repeat the question a little louder.

'Well now, I guess that would be when my mother died. That was 1930.' Calum did not hesitate with the date. 'I don't think anybody's been in it since then.'

There was a pause.

'She could have left it before then herself, of course, but she never did. Didn't want to. Always said they'd have to carry her out. That's what they did, in the end.'

'I suppose, if it was her home…'

'Oh sure, sure.' Calum chuckled. 'She was tough. Nobody was gonna make her leave.'

At that point Iain heard a voice speaking to Calum.

'Well boy, I gotta go. The big boss says I gotta take my food.'

'It's been good to speak to you.'

'You too, son, you too.'

Another voice came on the line, a woman's.

'Hi. Is that Iain? I'm Beth, Calum's daughter. Your mom's cousin.'

'Hi.'

'I don't want to spoil his fun. It's just that he needs to get his food now. He'd sit and talk all day if he could, but he's gotta do his routine or he gets sick. I have to keep telling him that.'

'Of course. That's no problem,' said Iain.

'Make sure you call back. He was enjoying himself. How's your mom?'

The conversation ended soon after. Iain smiled as he hung up the phone. The old man had sounded alert and there was already an image in Iain's head of a smiling face with a thatch of white hair. He was looking forward to speaking to him again.

He sat up until the early hours with his mother. Open before them was the old suitcase that had held the family's memories for as long as he could remember. Photographs, wallets of loose negatives, postcards, cards for birthdays and anniversaries. The passage of so many lives, haphazardly scattered. His father's sixty-five years in frozen fragments. In his christening shawl, held by his solemn-faced mother. The smiling lad in his Sabbath best. The young soldier staring intently at the camera with something of his mother's solemnity. Standing with his new wife, his hair thickly greased, a rare sight of his squint teeth through a smile, very thin in his uniform. In the first colour photo he stands with his wife, sons and daughter at a cousin's wedding. The hair is greying now as he squints in the late afternoon sunshine, once again dressed in his best. Iain could remember his mother knotting his father's tie for him that day. And one of the final ones, holding the hands of two of his grandchildren. He wears a cardigan and he is smiling, a smile Iain knew so well. It took so long for him to be natural before a camera, but then the children brought out the best in him. It was one of the last ever taken of him.

In the changing styles of their day, he examined images of the passing generations, all linked by blood and shared history.

'There's Calum,' said Mary, pulling a stiff, cardboard-mounted photo from among the pile. 'That's him just before he left.'

Iain had seen the photograph before, but never really studied it. The young man looking back at him, really no more than a boy, was slighter than he'd thought. His wavy, dark hair was combed into a precise side parting and the dark eyes seemed uncomfortable in the stare of the camera lens. He wore a three-piece suit and polished boots. A watch-chain looped from a buttonhole to the pocket of his waistcoat.

'And there's Iain and Finlay, the two who were lost.'

Finlay looked an altogether more confident character than Calum. He had the same colouring as his brother and the same wavy hair, but he was bigger, with his square face seemingly resisting a smile. He wore the uniform of the Royal Navy, a dark, knitted sweater with a blue and white kerchief draped over his shoulders and knotted at his breastbone. A white lanyard emerged from underneath and was tied in the same naval knot. He stood behind the eldest brother Iain, who was seated on a chair wearing the same uniform. He too had the same dark colouring, and bore a thick black moustache.

'Oh, would you look at them,' his mother sighed. 'So young. Just boys.'

Iain slept better than he'd expected. He'd enjoyed a couple of malts as he and his mother reminisced into the deep hours of the night, the peat fire degrading into ash and spreading warmth all around them. He wasn't troubled by images of skeletons buried in white sheets, nor by memories of lads who had been so harshly robbed of their youth.

Chapter Five

A FRIED BREAKFAST in bed might not make for a healthy heart, but it certainly made for a happy one. Mary was enjoying spoiling him and Iain was taking pleasure from it.

Yvonne always complained his mother had ruined him and she'd been right enough. When they had first married, he had been quite hopeless domestically and it was the source of most of their early rows. He reflected ruefully that there was really no excuse for his laziness; it was only what he had been used to. His mother would even tidy his flat when she visited Glasgow and then the mess would accumulate until her next trip.

He knew at the time he should be ashamed, but he never was. There was too much going on in his life; drinking in student bars, going to see bands, sometimes studying. Food had been no more than fuel, usually anything from a can. But he had developed one speciality of his own. Tuna fish curry was not to everyone's taste, but it had been his treat to himself when he couldn't afford a proper takeaway. He couldn't remember where he'd picked up on the recipe, although doubtless it had been in some bar. He still shuddered at the thought of the first time he'd made it. Yoghurt was a key ingredient, he'd been told, but he'd made the mistake of thinking that any yoghurt would do. His tuna fish curry with strawberries would not make it into any recipe book.

Perhaps it was only now that he fully appreciated how

fortunate his generation had been. The photographs of boys in battledress were sobering. He remembered so many of these lads as old men in the district when he was growing up. Despite it all, they were mostly free of rancour and resentment. In his memory they were men of warmth and dignity whose pride was borne, not in the survival of their own experiences, but in the opportunities being explored by their children and grandchildren. They must have had their moments of bitterness, but Iain could not recall ever seeing or hearing it.

For himself, there was almost a regression in sitting in his bed with a tray of fried food and hot tea on his lap. He could savour it but it couldn't last and he wouldn't want it to. His mother knew that too, but she was enjoying his company in the house. It took her mind off other worries.

Life was lonely for her now. Few of her own generation still lived in the village, most were either dead or had departed to other places. People didn't call into each other's houses like they used to. It was rare enough even to see them walking in the road. Her life had spanned the change from one culture to another, from the old ways of community to the more comfortable but more isolated times of television and motor car. She could go a full day and more without speaking to anyone face to face. How she missed her husband. Just to hear a voice after the television had been switched off, when the only sound was the creaks of the house settling for the night. The solitude would slink up on her and pull her down, so she kept herself busy.

The church, with its clubs, friends and services was the axis of her life now, although visits from her children and grandchildren were the highlights. It was good to have Iain with her, to know that in the depth of night, when she felt most alone, there was someone nearby. Not that she would ever disturb him; just the thought was comfort enough.

Within an hour of rising, he was on his way back to the old house. The sun was behind him as he walked towards the sea. The colours of the bay were sharp in the clear light of morning, bold blues and greens so different from the shadows and golden shades of dusk.

His wellingtons scrunched on the stones and gravel, sometimes sending a chip bouncing and skittering ahead of him. A ditch ran down one side of the road where the land sloped up and away from the village, losing itself in the moorland. A slab of flat rock had been placed across the ditch at the point where Iain left the road for the old house. His comings and goings in recent days had flattened the grass around it, but until then it had been overgrown and hidden. It had taken a while to find it. It was very useful for getting his barrow across and would be even more so when he had to start removing the accumulation of debris that was building up.

The dew slicked his boots as he strode up the path he'd worn. He paused at the entrance of the house. As he stepped forward, there was a frantic rustle and clatter and a sudden movement inside. Iain's hands shot out in alarm, his heart kicking against his chest, then a sheep leapt out, its hind legs tripping on obstacles, its flanks thumping off the sides of the doorway.

As it scrambled away up the hillside, its tail bobbing, Iain heaved a deep breath. His hands were shaking and he consciously had to steady his breathing. In the couple of seconds it had taken for him to realise that it was a sheep, incoherent thoughts had plundered his mind. He reproached himself for being so uptight.

As he walked through the doorway, he looked immediately to his right. Nothing had changed from the previous night. The mound of earth lay undisturbed at the fire opening and he could see a patch of rag.

Another sound crept up on him. Footsteps coming through the grass. Iain moved back to the entrance.

'Hi, cove.' It was Neilie. 'Christ, you've started early. I thought you'd still be in your bed getting spoilt by your ma.'

Iain sighed again, his heart still jumping.

'Aye, well there's a lot to do.'

Neilie's eyes settling on the mound of earth dumped outside.

'What are you digging all this for? Leave it. I'll get one of the diggers down here. Maybe not today like I said, but I'll get it shifted in no time.'

'It's okay,' said Iain. 'I said there's no need for that.'

'Don't be so daft. Just leave it to me. I'll get it dug and cleared.'

'No, really Neilie, it's fine.'

'It's no problem.'

'I know, but... well, you can't get a digger in here.'

'Just pull down a bit more of the wall there. It wouldn't take a morning. I'll do it myself and you can take the day off.'

'Thanks, but I don't mind it.'

'There's tons here,' persisted Neilie. 'It'll take you days, weeks.'

'Thanks, cove,' said Iain firmly, 'but I want to do it. It's part of the challenge.'

Neilie looked at him steadily in silence for a few moments.

'Let me help you. The rate you're going at, we'll all be

dead by the time you're finished.'

'No. Really.'

'Daft bugger,' said Neilie, turning away abruptly.

Iain sighed. It was always the same with Neilie. It was his way, or no way. Iain walked after him. Neilie was sitting on a rock, placing tobacco carefully onto a cigarette paper.

'Look, I appreciate the offer. You know that,' he said. 'Yes, it'd be quicker and easier, but that's not why I'm here.'

Neilie concentrated on using his finger to spread the tobacco evenly, balancing his tobacco tin carefully on his knees. He licked the paper and completed rolling a thin cigarette. Then he pressed the stray strands of tobacco back into the roll-up, put it in his mouth and closed the tin. He took a box of matches from his dungaree pocket and struck one, protecting it from the breeze in his cupped hand, and lit his fag. The tip burned brightly as he inhaled, a cloud of smoke billowing away from him in the wind.

'Neilie,' said Iain with a plea for understanding in his voice. 'C'mon.'

Neilie took another draw, his hands almost obscuring the lower half of his face. He turned to look at Iain.

'Why are you here, exactly?' he asked sourly.

'What?' responded Iain, taken aback.

'The house. It's not why you're here. That's what you just said. Well I'm asking, why are you here?'

'I told you.'

'You told me some crap about rebuilding the house. I keep telling you that you can't live in it unless you do the job properly. Everybody else thinks you're daft. Then when I try to help you, you don't want to know. You say it's not why you're here. So I'm asking, why are you here?'

'It is for the house. I just need to do it myself.'

Neilie's tone was one of controlled anger.

'You're messed up. Don't try to mess us all up as well.'
Then he stood up and strode quickly away.

'What the hell are you on about?' demanded Iain.

Neilie ignored him. Iain took a couple of paces after
him, but then held himself in check. It would be better to
deal with this when Neilie calmed down. What had set
him off? The two of them had gone out for a pint the night
Iain had come home and there had been no hostility. What
had sparked it now? Perhaps Neilie had drunk too much
the night before and was feeling the hangover.

Iain cursed in exasperation, and turned back into the
house. The grave appeared to be undisturbed. He stood
over it, wondering what to do. The sensible thing would
be to alert the authorities right away, but his curiosity
incited him to find out more first.

His digging tools were standing upright inside the old
chimney and he grasped the spade and thrust it into the
ground, shovelling away more stones. Clumps of peat and
clay stuck to it and then fell off with the motion. Again he
did it, and again, throwing the earth to one side, exposing
more of the sheeting. Previously his digging had been rapid
and aggressive, almost feverish. Now it was slower, more
measured, but it didn't take too long for the full length of
the remains to be exposed. Using the knife again, he split
the cloth wider until the skeleton took on a complete,
recognisable form.

The body had been laid to rest in a formal manner, on
its back, the arms crossed on its breast and the legs fully
extended. Over time it had settled awkwardly, twisted
towards the right, with the distortion more exaggerated
from the waist down. It was difficult to estimate its size
with any accuracy because of its position and the sheeting
around it. It was certainly no bigger than he was, a couple

of inches short of six feet.

He sat up on the wall again. A decision had to be made. The more he considered calling the police, the more he persuaded himself against it. Any police investigation would be unlikely to yield anything and would just hold him back from a project that he felt had started so well. As he sluiced the idea around in his head, he convinced himself that he should be able to discover the explanation himself. And if he didn't, then he could call in the police. His initial alarm had been replaced by the tingle of a thrill at the prospect of finding out the real story of the bones.

A chill in the air made him look seaward. Dark clouds were hanging on the horizon. Rain was on its way, heavy rain by the looks of it. That would restrict any further digging. The bones would need to be protected from the elements, but he didn't want to fill in the hole again. There was nothing nearby that he could use.

Mary was surprised by his early return. She was weeding in her garden, lost among the lupins that were her favourite. When he appeared she began to pull herself up, her arm on her knee.

'I wasn't expecting you so soon.'

'I'm just calling for something. I'm going back down.'

Iain was already walking past her to the barn.

It had been built by his father in the 1950s. Iain recalled how important he'd felt, helping him mix the cement. He hadn't been in the barn in a decade or more. Hardly anyone had since his father's death. His brother and sister, Kenny and Christine, refused to allow their children to go into it because they thought it unsafe.

Iain put his shoulder to the door and pushed hard. It opened more easily than he'd expected, scraping across the stone floor. In his childhood, his father's sheepdogs

would have greeted him with bright eyes, wagging tails
and excited barks. There had been several of them down
through the years, all border collies of differing
temperaments and personalities. None had been allowed
in the house. The barn, where most of them had been born,
had been their home.

Meg had been a particular favourite; a calm, sensible
bitch when working with the sheep and an utterly devoted
companion to his father for more than ten years. Sheila
and Lucy were two others that Iain remembered fondly,
not forgetting the utterly useless Caber. He was highly-
strung and easily distracted, with a lolling tongue that gave
him a rather stupid look, but he was a great playmate. His
weakness was that he chased anything and everything with
equal enthusiasm, sheep, rabbits and cars. It was the latter
proclivity that led to his early demise.

The old cow stalls were still against the back wall, three
of them, although he could only remember ever having
two cows at any one time. His father, in his denim
dungarees, checked shirt and worn, flat cap, would sit on
a small stool pulling at their udders. He could almost hear
the tinny sound of the newly drawn milk spraying into the
pail. Iain had never quite got the hang of it himself. His
father could fill the pail with creamy, foaming, warm milk,
but he always struggled to make even half a pail before
the cows got impatient and sore.

An open loft covered half the roof area and the wooden
ladder was still there. Iain wasn't confident it would still
bear his weight. And there on one of the crossbeams was
the worn, knotted rope he and Kenny used to swing on.
The fun they had here! This had been their adventure
playground when the weather curtailed outdoor activities.
Once, Kenny had sent their father sprawling when he

swung from the rope, expecting Iain through the door. Iain could still see the horror on Kenny's face as his leap took him full force into his father. The two of them had sprawled along the floor and Kenny had got the thrashing of his life. Painful at the time, but it always left the two of them helpless with laughter when they reminisced.

The barn had been their refuge so often when the Sabbatarianism of their parents and their community had denied them television or games. They would play furtive games of football, or listen to the pop charts on their radio. Christine had grown wise to this and made a lot of money out of the bribes they paid her to keep quiet.

He'd had his first kiss here, with Catriona, and his first cigarette with the boys. It all rushed back to him as he opened the door.

But the place was not abandoned. Through the dust that swirled in the sunshine streaming in, Iain could see that his mother continued to use it for storage. Opposite the cow stalls there were stacks of plastic sacks of fertiliser and peat. A lawnmower stood in one corner.

'What are you looking for?'

His mother was pushing past him.

'I didn't know you still used this place.'

'Just things for the garden.'

'That's peat, Ma. You told me you bought it from that fellow in town, but you're still cutting it yourself, aren't you?'

'And what of it?' Mary asked defensively.

'Nothing. You kept that to yourself. Where d'you get it?'

'The same place as always.'

'But that's miles away. How d'you get it home here?'

'Neilie helps me now and again. He's very good to me.'

'So you've been bringing home the peats all those years and you never let on?' Iain couldn't keep the smile from his voice.

'I'm not going to pay someone to bring my peats when I can get my own just as well.' Mary was clearly irritated that she'd been found out. 'Anyway, what is it you wanted?'

'The tarpaulin. The one the old man used to use to cover the peat stack.'

He knew that his mother would not have disposed of it. Despite the improvement in their prosperity, she was of a generation that was reluctant to get rid of anything that might have potential use. She stood looking around the barn.

'Now, I saw it a while ago. Where was it?'

She stood for some time with her hand on her cheek, trying to remember. Then she was scrambling up onto the pile of plastic sacks. Iain stood behind her in case she lost her balance. When she began tugging at something behind them, he climbed up beside her and helped pull. Eventually the bulkily folded tarpaulin was in his hands. Mary was puffing a little.

'So what else have you been hiding?' he teased her.

'More than you'll know,' she answered defiantly. And with that, she turned and headed out of the barn back to the house.

By the time Iain had stuffed the tarpaulin into his car, she had cooled down.

'I've made a pot of tea if you want some,' she called.

The two of them sat on the window-ledge of the house, sheltered from the strengthening breeze. She told him about her plants, pointing to particular favourites, the roses and the yellow forsythia, the broom bush. Each one had its story. Once or twice she asked, 'Now who gave me that one?' before moving on. Her little garden was her domain, where she need please no one but herself.

'What else does Neilie do for you?' Iain asked eventually.

'He's just very good to me. He gives me runs here and there. Him and Catriona both. Now don't you get started on the peats again. I've cut them all my life and I'll keep cutting them while I'm able.'

'I get that. He just never said anything to me about it.'

'Maybe I asked him not to because someone might create a fuss,' replied Mary pointedly.

'How's he been?'

'What d'you mean? You've seen him yourself.'

'I just wondered if you'd seen any change in him. Catriona thinks he's a bit down.'

'Neilie is always the same to me.'

Iain finished his tea and drove back down to the old house. He needed both arms to carry the tarpaulin and it dislodged a couple of stones as he pushed it through the doorway. The first clatter made him look round sharply. What was there to fear? He knew what was in there and yet he couldn't control his nervousness.

The mouth of the bay was all but obscured by the approaching downpour. Hastily, Iain stretched the sheeting over the hole and weighted it down with heavy stones. The rain began spattering down in large globules and pools immediately began to form in the folds, but eventually he was satisfied that the bones were protected both from the elements and from the curious – human or animal. The skull had been the last part to be covered, its image burning onto his mind like a photographic exposure.

'Who are you?' he asked aloud.

Chapter Six

BY THE TIME he returned home, his mother had gone out. With the house to himself, he could think through what to do. He had never been one for rush judgements, preferring to mull things over and over in his head.

He picked up the local paper. Amid the community news, he came across a report of an archaeological dig in Uig. Archaeologists were forever on the island. There was such a long history of human habitation, and so much of it was still not understood. The renowned Calanais Stones had been uncovered more than one hundred and fifty years before and had been erected three thousand years before that, yet there was still no definitive understanding of their purpose and design.

So many peoples had settled on the Hebrides, Vikings, early Christians, Picts; unknown peoples from the Iron Age and before had known this place. The dry sands and the sodden peatlands still yielded enticing glimpses of the past. History hunters came in their droves.

Normally, Iain would not have given the article a second glance, but it gave him an idea. Satisfied with his plan of action, he passed the remainder of the afternoon lost in thought, with the rain splattering comfortingly against the dormer window of his room.

There would be many more days like this to come, when the weather would keep him indoors. He realised he'd forgotten such days when he'd made his plans for coming home. He had envisaged working on the house, going long walks, heading up to the hotel when he felt like it, maybe even taking up the fishing again. Now questions and doubts came for the first time. Who would he go to the hotel with? Most of his other friends were living away, the few who remained were tied by families and jobs. Their lives had diverged and the friendships of youth would not be easily resurrected. The freedoms of this new life might be lonely ones.

He was dozing off when the phone rang. It was Mary.

'Where are you?' she asked.

'Well obviously I'm at home, Ma, I've just answered the phone.'

'Didn't I ask you to come for me when you were ready?'

'No.'

'Well, would you mind? It's bucketing down.'

'Where are you?'

'Agnes's of course. Just when you're ready.'

The windscreen wipers could barely clear the rain and the interior was misting from the dampness of his clothes, wet from the short sprint to the car. Nothing would do when he arrived, but that he should say hello to his mother's old friend. Agnes MacLennan was so pleased to see him, her leathery, lined skin creasing in delight at the sight of him. She had been his Sunday School teacher once and had always taken such an interest in the family. Her living-room was gloomy with dated furniture. Fresh peats smoked on the fire and the air carried the lingering tang of cooked fish.

He must have a cup of tea and of course he couldn't refuse some cake. Two small blobs of curdled milk swirled in his cup. Yvonne would have gagged, but it didn't bother Iain. Maybe the milk wasn't so fresh, but the welcome was sincere.

'And how are you getting on with the house?' Agnes asked.

'Making progress.'

'My, but it's a hard job you've given yourself there, a' ghraidh. They closed that house up when I was young.'

'Do you remember that?'

'Oh yes. I think it was Alasdair closed it, your great-uncle. When his mother died, there was no more reason to keep it open. My, but people were glad to get out of the old houses. So smoky and dark. I wonder what they would make of you wanting to stay in it again.'

'They'd think his head needed looking at,' his mother said, and the two women laughed.

Iain didn't object to the gentle teasing. He was intrigued to discover what else Agnes could recall.

'That was all they would do? Turn the key and walk away?'

'Well, yes. What else would they do? Over the years, I suppose people must have taken things away from it. Wood and such.'

'Sad times,' observed his mother aloud.

'Oh my, yes. Closing the house must have been sad. But once the old lady was gone, no one else wanted to live there. She would never have left it.'

'Why not?' asked Iain.

'Well, it was the family home. All her memories were there. She just flat wouldn't leave it. I still remember Alasdair taking the cow through the village.'

'The cow?'

'Yes, a' ghraidh. There always seemed to be a cow getting sold when someone died, especially when it was an older man. It would be too much for the widow to look after. I always thought it was very sad. Not Annie Oran.

She always kept a beast, right up until she died. She was a strong woman.'

'I didn't know that was her nickname, Annie Oran,' said Iain.

'I must have told you that,' said Mary.

'Oh, but they say she was a beautiful singer,' said Agnes. 'Even in her old age you could hear her sing the psalms so clearly. Some said she had the best voice heard on the island.'

'And do you remember Calum, her son?'

'My, yes. He went to Canada. There was nothing for him here. That was the way for so many of them. The boys came back from the trenches and found the land they'd been promised just wasn't there. No land and no jobs. There were these advertisements in the *Gazette* offering jobs in Canada for men, and for the women too.' Agnes chuckled. 'I was all for going myself, but my father said I was too young and when I think about it, he was right. There was a man came round the island taking names of people to emigrate to Canada. I remember the meeting here. There was a lot of them there to hear what he had to say. They filled the hall. And afterwards they were all for going. Calum was there, I'm sure. He must have been.'

'And Finlay?'

There was a momentary pause.

'No, I don't think so. But Calum was there. He went after all.'

Iain detected something in her hesitation over Finlay.

'Where would Finlay have been?'

Agnes shook her head gently and made a whispering sound with her breath.

'Finlay was different. It was the war. He was never the same after it. Folk used to say he'd been such a nice lad, friendly, and good to his mother and father. But the war changed him. It changed them all, I'm sure, but you really saw it with Finlay.'

'What d'you remember of him?'

'I never spoke to him, didn't really see much of him. Nobody did. He was very dark. I don't mean in his looks, but there just seemed to be a cloud over him. I don't know if I ever saw the man smile. Not like Calum, who was always so cheery. Calum was a bit older than me, but I always had, you know, a wee thing for him.' Agnes giggled girlishly. 'Oh, but Calum was quite the looker with his wavy hair, and always laughing. His brother was so different. I remember saying something to my mother one day about him scaring me and she was quite short with me. "You don't know what that poor man has been through," she said. She told me that it was a blessing for his mother that he was still here. Well, I'm sorry to say it, but I wasn't so sure.'

'My mother said the same,' said Mary. 'That the war changed him. He was her older brother, of course, and he had been so kind to her before, but I think she became a bit fearful of him. She said he had some temper. And sometimes she could hear him crying in his bed.'

'I'm sure they could do things for them now, but then they were just left to get on with it,' Agnes said.

'My mother said that's why Calum took him to America, to see if he could make a go of things there, but the poor soul didn't last long.'

Agnes nodded. 'How often did I hear my mother speak of the *Metagama*, the ship that took them all away from Stornoway.'

'Well, not all of them,' Mary corrected her. 'Calum joined it from Stornoway, but Finlay had been in Glasgow for a time, and he joined it from there. So did some others. That was the first time I was ever in town, to see them off on the *Metagama*. I thought it was so exciting. There was pipers and dancing. I'd never seen so many folk, all there with their cases and their hats and coats. But it was sad too. The mothers and fathers waving cheerio to their sons and daughters. There were a lot of hankies used that day, I can tell you. Of course, they were gone for good. Most of them, anyway. It was all so sad, but probably it was the best thing that could have happened for most of them. It was possible to make a good life over there. I suppose they must have had their thoughts, though.'

It was nearly two hours later before Iain and his mother got home. As soon as they were in, she went for a lie down.

The ocean and sky were leaden, but he wanted to go to the old house. Agnes's stories had brought the people who had lived there back to life. He put on his waterproof and wellingtons and went out into the wind. Beyond the village, the sense of isolation was like a peaceful pool and the slightest disturbance could be sensed. As he approached the house he felt something had changed. He quickened his pace towards the last bend.

A small, brown tent was pitched on the leeward side of the house. Iain approached cautiously. It was as if his home had been broken into. Strange that he should feel that way. He had seen plenty of tents pegged just beyond the sandy beaches. Backpackers came from all points, drawn by the mystery and the majesty of the landscape.

This tent, being so close to the house, made him edgy. What exploring had been done? What had been seen?

No one was inside the walls of the house. Had a corner

of the tarpaulin been moved, or had he not laid it properly? As he came back through the door, a figure loomed suddenly before him. Iain jumped back, his hands raised reflexively.

The figure was also startled. It was a man, younger than Iain, with unruly hair and a beard that needed trimming. He wore a woollen jumper with holes in places, jeans and well-worn hiking boots.

'I'm sorry,' he said in a strong accent. 'My tent.'

Iain began to relax.

'I'm Peter. I'm from West Germany.'

Iain replied, touching his chest, 'I'm from here.'

'Ah,' nodded Peter. 'It is a good place. I did not know that this belonged to anyone. Is it okay if I stay?'

'Of course it is.'

'Yeah, thanks. I have been here before. With my girlfriend. We find it by luck, ja? Lisa liked it very much. So peaceful.' He pondered for a moment, then laughed. 'Not like Düsseldorf.'

'No,' smiled Iain, 'It's not like anywhere else. Is she with you, your girlfriend?'

'No.' Peter looked as if he was about to say something, but then dropped his head and just repeated, 'No.'

Iain didn't pursue it.

'Your English is very good,' he said, changing the subject.

'Thank you. I like to travel like this and it is good to speak English. Also, I learned a little at school.'

'Well, it's very good. When did you arrive?'

'Not long. I make my tent and then go to y'know... toilet.'

'You have to make sure the wind is in the right direction.'

It took the German a moment to understand, but when he did the two men chuckled together.

'The wind,' said Peter gesturing around him. 'Always the wind.'

'Always,' agreed Iain. 'So, how often have you come here?'

'This is my fifth time.'

'Five times you've travelled from Düsseldorf to here?'

'Not always from Germany. Always I am travelling and come from different places. It is the edge of the map, you know. I stop here and then I go back. This house... how old is it?'

'More than a hundred years, anyway. It used to be that all the houses were clustered together over there,' Iain pointed to a knoll that stood slightly higher than the others around it. 'That's where the people lived for a long, long time. But there was never any guarantee they would be able to stay on the land. Then they were finally given promises that they could settle here. That's when they built these houses.'

'It looks as if it has been here for all time. How could they move such big stones?'

'Like the pyramids, eh?' They both laughed. 'It would take them a long time and sometimes they had to break the stones down.'

'A big job also.'

'What they did was build peat fires on the rocks and burn them over a day or two. Eventually the rock would get so hot it would crack and then they could break it more easily.' The scale of the task registered with both men. 'You seem very interested.'

'I like to know about places. I think it must be very good to know where you come from. Where I am from, it is a city, and you don't know so much about what happened before. After the last war, my grandfather and grandmother lived in Düsseldorf, but I don't know where they came from before that. I don't even know where they stayed in the city. I know where my father was born, but that is all.'

'I'm sure you could find out.'

'Yes, maybe. But it might not be there any more. In the cities they build and build. It always changes. Especially in Germany. And I don't speak much to my parents. They wanted me to work, but that is not for me. Not yet.'

Spits of rain began to fall.

'I'd best be going,' said Iain. 'You'll need to get organised for the night.'

'Oh that is easy. My tent is up and I have a stove.' Peter hesitated. 'This is your house, ja?'

'Yes, I suppose it is.'

Peter looked enquiringly at Iain.

'It was the old family home many years ago. I'm hoping to rebuild it.'

Peter assessed what Iain had said.

'That will change things very much.'

'Oh, I don't know.'

'When will you begin?'

'I already have.'

'Already?' said Peter in surprise.

'Just digging.'

'Where?'

'In the house. Clearing the floor.'

Peter walked through the doorway and looked at the tarpaulin. Iain watched him uncertainly.

'I'm sorry,' Peter said gesturing with his hand. 'I come here so often and it never changes. That is why I like it so much. Now it changes.'

Iain said nothing. He had warmed to this stranger's company, but now he was irritated by his apparent disapproval. Peter obviously realised this and attempted to explain.

'You must excuse me. I'm sorry. I was surprised a little. And Lisa...'

A quizzical look came onto Iain's face.

'My girlfriend, Lisa. You asked if she was here. She is not. She is dead.'

Iain nodded slowly. 'I'm sorry,' he said quietly.

'This place was very special to her and that is why it is still special to me. We had good times here. But now if it changes, it will not be as it was when she saw it. Do you understand?'

Iain nodded again.

'Of course, everything changes,' said Peter in a conciliatory tone, smiling nervously.

'It's okay,' said Iain, finding himself at something of a loss.

'She wanted to always come here again, but she never did.'

Iain sensed that Peter did not want to be left alone just yet.

'You must miss her.'

'Excuse me?'

'You wish she was still with you?'

'Ja. Every day. It was very sad. She took something bad and I couldn't help her.' Peter hung his head for a few moments. 'When I come here I am with her again.'

The two men stood silently for a few moments, unaware of the rain.

'I will see you tomorrow?' said Iain finally.

'Yes. Maybe I help you,' smiled Peter.

'Have a good night.'

'Good night.'

As he walked back up the road, Iain thought over their conversation. It said much for Peter's devotion to his Lisa that he would travel back to the village just to feel closer to her. He couldn't imagine Yvonne ever doing that. She would never return here again. It had been difficult enough to persuade her to come even when they were together.

His first reaction of annoyance that there was an intruder in his special place had been dispelled. What was undeniably disconcerting, though, was Peter's intensely negative reaction to his plans. 'When I come here I am with her again,' he had said. What exactly had he meant by that? Iain had taken it in a spiritual context, but perhaps not. He resolved to be rational. If Peter was still there tomorrow and nothing had been disturbed, then he could be sure that Peter was just what he said he was: a man grieving for his lost love.

Chapter Seven

THE RAIN CONTINUED sweeping down through the evening and Iain grew restless. Mary was still in her bed when he got home and he made dinner, heating a pie he found in the fridge. She was delighted with his efforts.

'So what are you going to do today?'

'Tonight?'

'Yes, tonight. I'm still half asleep,' she smiled. 'It's not much of a night for outside. Are you going to the hotel?'

'I don't think so, everyone will be busy. I'll maybe head up to Neilie's.'

He was still needled by their encounter that morning. He could stew over it or he could confront his friend and sort it out.

Catriona answered the door wearing a baggy old sweatshirt, yet still she looked lovely.

'Hi,' said Iain cheerfully. 'Is the man in?'

'No,' Catriona replied. 'He's away up to the hotel.'

Her curt manner took him aback.

'Is everything okay?'

She rubbed the back of her hand against her damp forehead.

'Yes,' she said distractedly, 'Just getting tidied up.'

'What's the matter?'

'Nothing.'

'Catriona,' said Iain knowingly.

'Och, he's gone off in a rage. Came home from his work and didn't even wait for something to eat. He's got the van with him as well.'

'Do you want me to get him?'

'No, I don't think so. That would just make him angrier.'

'Why? What's got into him?'

'I don't know, I really don't know.'

Iain stepped into the large, open-plan kitchen. Catriona turned away from him towards the sink. He took a seat at the breakfast bar and waited for her to speak. When she did, she still didn't look at him.

'This is what it's been like ever since Rob's mother died. It's got worse since he heard you were coming home. There's no talking to him. I'm scared to say anything in case he blows up. Then it's off to the hotel and he comes back in a state.' She was on the verge of tears.

'He hasn't done anything, has he? He hasn't…'

'No, no, nothing like that. Just growls at me. And some of the things he says.'

'Like what?'

'It's all nonsense. But nasty.' She looked so vulnerable. Iain moved towards her, his arms open to comfort her.

'Oh don't do that for goodness sake! If he came in now he'd go mad.' Now the tears did flow.

'What's this all about?' Iain stepped back.

She wiped her eyes with a rumpled paper hankie.

'I saw him this morning and he was wound up.'

'That's what set him off. He said you'd refused his help and when I told him that maybe you just wanted to be on your own, he went off about my taking your side and all the rest of it.'

'We've got to sort this out.'

'Oh no, Iain,' pleaded Catriona, 'Leave it.'

'He won't know I've been here. He knows I'd know where to find him.'

Catriona didn't respond. Nor did she resist when he gave her a hug. Momentarily he felt the contours of her body against his. He kissed her hair and let her cry. It was still there for him. Still there, so strong.

She filled his mind all through the drive to the hotel, a converted two-storey school house with a bar, lounge, restaurant and a few rooms upstairs. Iain remembered the fuss when it first opened. The minister had condemned it as the Devil's work, but for many it was a deliverance of a different kind.

Before, those with a thirst had to travel to town more than twenty miles away. Organising lifts or accommodation could make that a complex operation. The alternatives were to get a carry-out or join the harder drinkers in the bothies dotted on well-used tracks on the moor, where some of the firewater produced could peel the throat.

The hotel controversy was history now. Iain had come here on his eighteenth birthday. He had felt so grown-up that night, walking into the bar among all the faces he knew in the district. He was one of them now. There were no similar recollections of leaving the place at the end of the evening, but Rob had seen him home. The racket of their return had shaken his mother from her bed. The scene was set for a showdown, but his father had recognised it as a rite of passage and told her to leave him be. There had been plenty other nights since then. If you wanted to drink with your pals, this was the place to come. Town was where you went if you wanted to chase girls.

He swung into the car park. Neilie's battered white van was there. The west side of the whitewashed building contained the lounge bar and the restaurant, where hotel guests could relax after a hard day's walking or fishing and local couples might come for a night out.

The east side of the building was illuminated by two wire-covered lights over a plain double door. Three translucent windows were set in the wall. This was the bar, the place the more serious drinkers were usually to be found; tradesmen slaking their thirst after a hard day's graft, the grime and dust of the job still clinging to them; lads having a bawdy night out; friends yarning. Those whose best friend was the bottle reaffirming their loyalty to it once again. Neilie would be here.

The smell of alcohol and smoke gushed out as soon as he opened the door. He half expected Puggy to be behind the bar, heavy and genial, hailing him with a 'How's the cove?' There was no Puggy, only a younger man he didn't recognise.

The bar ran the full length of the far wall. On the gantry were whisky blends and black rum, Trawler Rum. A trade bottle of vodka stood beneath them and the malt whiskies next to that. Pumps lined the bar, Tennent's beer or lager, Blackthorn cider and Guinness. If any customer wanted something different, and that was unusual, the bar staff had to bring it through from the lounge bar.

A clutch of faces turned towards the door to assess the new arrival. One or two worthies from the village returned his self-conscious nods. He knew they would soon be confiding to each other in the Gaelic, 'That's Murdo Martin's son. The one doing the building at the old house.'

Neilie sat at a stained formica table, a half-full pint in front of him. Drying rings of froth showing the dropping level after each mouthful. His head shot back quickly and another whisky went down.

Iain walked over and sat down opposite him. Neilie looked up, his face still grimacing from the whisky. He took a long gulp of beer.

'Want another?' asked Iain.

Neilie washed the beer around his mouth and didn't reply.

'I'm getting one anyway. D'you want one?'

Neilie shrugged.

The barman, who looked like a boy Catriona had baby-sat when they were teenagers, served him efficiently with two pints and two drams, but without recognition. Iain wrapped his fingers around all four drinks and carried them back to the table. The cold beer tasted good.

'What's wrong?' he asked directly.

'Clear off,' Neilie answered dismissively.

'No. This morning. What was that all about?'

'I came here for a drink in peace.'

'Neilie, you're my oldest pal,' Iain persisted. 'What's got into you?'

The only response was a pained expression.

'Look, stop messing about. If I've done something then tell me.'

Neilie swept up his whisky, downed it, and suddenly thrust his face low towards Iain.

'You've done nothing, right? It's me. It's me.'

'Why, what have you done? This isn't like you.'

'I've got things on my mind, that's all.' His initial aggression seemed to dissipate.

'Tell me about it,' encouraged Iain.

'Why? Did you say anything to me about Yvonne? No, nothing.'

'I wasn't here to say anything.'

'That's you alright. Never there when it matters.'

'What?'

'I'll tell you things if you want. Sure I will. This whole thing about the old house. Madness. You've no plans, you've not got the tools, no idea what you're doing. You'll never do it. All this trying to change things. I'm sick of people trying to do that. I thought you would be too. Just leave things alone.'

He slurped a mouthful from his pint.

'People left these houses because they weren't fit to live in any more. Why do people seem to think that the past was such a great place? It was tough. Folk couldn't wait to escape it. Leave the past alone. What's done is done.'

'I'm not trying to change anything.'

'Things are changing just by you being here.'

'What d'you mean by that?'

'Just leave it.'

'This isn't just about me coming home, is it? There's more.'

'Oh, and who have you been talking to? Cat been pouring out her troubles, has she? Might have known.'

'Cat's said nothing. She didn't need to.'

Neilie sat upright, almost falling back off the stool.

'You think? Well let me tell you something Iain boy, I don't think Cat-Rion-A could care less. Not her, cove. She married the wrong one and she knows it. She knows it and she regrets it. I know it too. She could have had the pick of us and she went for me. Rob was gone, and that was my fault too.'

Iain sat listening intently, barely moving. Neilie looked unsteadily at him through heavy lids.

'Oh, but we're quiet now, cove. Don't want to talk now, eh? Don't like what you're hearing? You know what you should do? You should stop pissing about in the past. Think on the present. Think of your ma. She needs you now.'

'What d'you mean?'

'You're asking me?'

Even through the drink, Neilie seemed to realise he had said too much and refused to say anything else that made any sense. He was intent on drinking himself to oblivion and it took persistence to get him to move, although he seemed quite steady as he walked to the door, shouting greetings to other drinkers. When the fresh air hit him, though, Iain had to support him to the van.

On the drive home Neilie bellowed a Gaelic drinking song, laughing to himself when he finished and clapping Iain on the shoulder.

'There you go, cove. There you go. Want another one?'

His resentment and anger seemed to have ebbed away. What had twisted him so?

The lights in the house were off when Iain pulled up. Neilie was giggling quietly as he helped him inside.

'Shh,' he said in a stage whisper.

Catriona came downstairs wrapped in a dressing-gown.

'Oh well, this is a surprise,' jested Neilie. 'I'm just going to my bed. And I'm sorry.'

Within the last sentence he moved from joking to tears. Iain helped him upstairs and Neilie was asleep almost as soon as his head fell onto the pillow.

Iain went back down to the kitchen.

'This is what it's like,' Catriona said. 'I usually pretend I'm asleep because he can be nasty with his mouth.'

Iain sat down. Catriona's face was drawn and pale.

'How was he with you?'

'He said a few things. Through the drink.'

'That's the only time he talks now. What did he say?'

'He's angry at me for coming back. I think maybe there's more, but that's all he'd say.'

The kettle clicked off and she turned to fill two mugs. Her shoulders were tense. He knew she was crying. Iain walked to her and put his hands on her neck.

'Is there more? Cat, I need to know.'

He brushed a damp strand of hair away from her face.

'Yes,' she said almost noiselessly. 'There is something else. Rob didn't die the way they say he did. What I don't know is exactly what did happen. And Neilie can't tell me.'

Chapter Eight

CATRIONA HAD TAINTED his thoughts, corroding the harmony he believed he had found. She had left him hanging. He had no recollection of the walk back to his mother's house, only of the doubts and sinister scenarios that flashed through his head. What was the truth?

Mary was still up when he got home. As she bustled off to make a pot of tea, he poured himself a generous dram and sat brooding over it. What had Catriona meant about Rob's death? Iain had relived those dreadful hours over and over again. The loss had partly formed the person he was now. And yet he was apparently to understand that he had been wrong about what had happened. Catriona's words would not leave him. 'Rob didn't die the way they say he did.' What did she know?

Tea-making was a fine art for his mother. Iain's tea was a scalded teabag with milk. Mary really brewed it. The leaves, and it had to be loose leaves, must settle, then rise and then settle again. It was a longer process, but the tea produced from her pot was an elixir, brown and strong. Even when he tried, Iain couldn't match its depth of taste, or its invigorating qualities.

She brought a cup through to him, asking brightly about his visit.

'We were speaking a lot about Rob.'

'Oh, my, my.'

'You remember when he died?'

She nodded her head sorrowfully.

'Did you ever hear anything more about it?'

Mary looked at him uncertainly.

'Did his mam ever say anything?'

'About what?'

'The way he died or anything.'

'Oh, I don't think she could bring herself to talk about that. Not without any remains. What was there to say? It was just so awful, to lose her boy, her only child like that.'

'You haven't heard anything different about what happened?'

She was confused by his questions.

'You were there, a' ghraidh.'

'Yes, I know. I just wondered if anything happened after I left? Nothing ever found?'

'You would have heard. I would have told you. No, they never found anything.'

'It's strange that there was never anything.'

'The sea has to be respected. It doesn't give up its secrets easily.'

'But they were so close to shore, weren't they? And yet nothing, not even a boot or a jacket.'

'I always wished they would find something. For his mother, so that she would know. But they never did.'

The doubts festered in his mind during the night. He resigned himself to waiting for the daylight, but sleep eventually smothered him unawares. Mary stirred him, bringing him breakfast in bed again, dismissing his protests.

Within the hour he was walking the quarter mile to the shore. At this time of the morning his senses seemed to come alive. True or not, he believed he could hear sounds from miles away; the lowing of a cow, the hum of a car on the road. The sea breeze swept the disturbed night from his head.

The road was empty. Sounds drifted to his ear; the exasperation of a mother trying to get her children ready for school; Braggan the Weaver working on a tweed in his loom shed. Braggan would be sitting on his wooden bench, his feet working mechanically on the heavy pedals, his eyes scanning the cloth, his hand occasionally flicking forward to remove a stray thread. Iain could hear the rhythmic clickety-clack of the shuttle being fired back and forth across the loom, trailing its thread through a fluctuating forest of yarn to create the hard-wearing cloth that was a trademark of the island.

These were the sounds of village life since ever he could remember. And the bed beneath it all, the ever-present whispering of the ocean.

The tent was still there, but there was no sign of Peter. He may have been inside, but the tent flap remained firmly zipped despite Iain calling his name. Inside the house, nothing seemed to have been disturbed. He wondered whether one or two of the rocks holding the tarpaulin had been moved, but he couldn't be certain.

A figure caught his eye, way over on top of the cliffs, but it dipped out of sight almost as soon as he saw it. He trained his eyes on the spot, but whoever it was didn't reappear. It was early for someone to be on the moor, but they would probably make themselves known soon enough. Perhaps it was the backpacker.

Iain removed some of the rocks and flapped back the tarpaulin. All was as he'd left it. He had formulated a plan to remove a bone so that it could be used to date the remains. Now, looking down on the skeleton, it seemed like a violation. It wasn't grave robbery perhaps, but his conscience complained that it was desecration. He stood for some moments, feet astride the grave, uncertain about what to do, or even what bone to choose. One of the ribs had fallen into the chest cavity and that made his mind up for him. He stooped quickly to pick it up, his fingers and forearm threatening to spasm as he did so, and placed it carefully on the grass. It took only moments to replace the tarpaulin and he made a quick mental note of where every stone was placed. He left, uncomfortable about what he had just done. The figure on the cliffs watched him as he trudged towards his car, placed the package in his boot and drove away.

He pulled off the road at Neilie and Catriona's, but there were no cars on the driveway, no sound from inside the house. They were gone. In the light of what had passed between them, Iain felt as if they had run away from him. Had Catriona said too much? Had she told Neilie? What more was there to tell?

He returned to his mother's house. All was quiet. He clicked on the kettle and rinsed the teapot of old leaves and as he was pouring the boiling water into the pot the door from the hall opened. His mother came in, looking pale and a little dishevelled.

'Oh Iain! You're up already?'

'What?'

Mary looked uncertain for a moment, then seemed to gather herself.

'Here, let me get that tea. Are you going down to the house?'

'I'm going to Uig.'

'Uig?' she asked in surprise.

'Aye, remember? I told you this morning. There's an archaeologist there I want to see.'

'Would you not be better phoning him? It's a journey to Uig.'

'It's a her, and I don't have a number. I saw in the *Gazette* that they're doing an excavation, and there's something I want them to see.'

'What?' she asked, giving him his tea.

'Something from the old house.'

'Well, let me see it. Surely I might have an idea. Folk are always running off to so-called experts. There's a lot of local knowledge to be used, you know.'

'I know, Ma, but I think it might be very old. And anyway, I haven't been over there in a while.'

'Will you be home for your dinner? I got some lovely trout from Tormod Mor.'

'Great. Was he out in the boat?'

'No, just from the rocks. He said he had a bag full of them.'

'You know I wouldn't miss that,' Iain assured her with a smile.

The island roads were gradually being widened to allow two cars to pass without stopping. They might be on the periphery of Europe, but that had its advantages when it came to regional aid. The road to Uig had yet to benefit and it reminded Iain of driving in his father's van along the single track roads with their passing places, the courtesies of pulling in and the acknowledgement of a casually raised finger from the steering wheel.

On the flat island, the hills of Uig could be seen from most parts, but it remained one of the most remote areas. Unlike most of Lewis, Uig had not escaped the clearances of the nineteenth century when the worth of man, woman and child was deemed as nothing. Much of the land was empty now, providing for modern travellers the peace and isolation that many sought.

He would have been quicker sailing down the coast to
Uig, but for Iain the road was the only way he knew.

The sands of Uig had revealed treasure before. The
Norse Chessmen found here captivated those who beheld
them in the museums of the mainland. Now, a dig was
going on after the discovery of an arrowhead from an even
earlier era.

Such was the expanse of empty beach, that it took Iain
some time to locate exactly where the dig was going on, a
quarter of a mile away, just where the smooth of the sands
mounted into the dunes of marram grass. Beneath his feet
the form of the sand changed constantly, from glass smooth
to the rippling sculpted by the motion of the seawater.

The sea was returning and would cover the sand again
soon. It didn't come in a rigid line of advance. White horses
curled in from the mouth of the bay, some sustaining their
momentum longer than others. As they broke onto the
sands, the clear water would slink up further and further.
Some sweeps would be cast beyond others and when they
slipped back towards the main body of water the two
would collide in an angular line, creating the phenomenon
of a wave crest that would zip across the beach at a speed
out of kilter with the languorous motion of the tide.

As Iain approached, a petite woman with dark, wild
hair appeared over a dune. She wore a heavy, knitted
sweater with the sleeves rolled up to just below her elbows,
jeans and hiking boots. There was a red kerchief knotted
around her neck and large silver earrings set with coloured
stones danced among her curls.

'Hello,' she said pleasantly in the neutral accent that
could be Scottish academia or English.

'Hello,' said Iain as he approached, carrying the
concealed bone.

She waited for him to say something more, her dark eyes watching him keenly. She had a sharp, intelligent face.

'I don't mean to trouble you,' he began. His mind had been so occupied with Catriona and Neilie that he hadn't given much thought to what he would say when he arrived here.

'You're an archaeologist, yes?'

She smiled and indicated the windbreakers that protected a pattern of small trenches where huddled figures were digging, scraping or measuring.

'One of many, yes.'

'I have something here. I thought maybe you'd like to look at it.'

Her eyes shifted to the cloth covering the bone. He lifted it towards her.

'It's a bone. Human I think.'

'Oh? Where did you find it?'

'Near my home.'

She took it from him, crouched down on the sand and began to unwrap it carefully.

'I was hoping you might be able to give me an idea of how old it is.'

'It looks human, although I can't be certain,' she said looking at it closely. 'What makes you so sure?'

'I know what animal bones are like,' he said.

'Of course,' she smiled apologetically. 'It doesn't look that old, certainly not of the age we have here. It's difficult for me to say without getting it analysed.'

Iain watched as she turned it in her hands.

'Where did you find it?'

'Near my home,' said Iain again, kneeling beside her.

'And where's that?'

'Just up the coast.'

'Maybe you should have taken this to the police.'

'Really? I didn't think to. There was only the one.'

'Just one bone on its own? Did you check if there were more?'

'Well…' Iain was reticent.

'You should maybe stop any digging you're doing. I honestly think it would be best to get this investigated properly.'

'No, there weren't any more,' Iain lied.

'That seems odd. It's from the rib. I can't imagine a rib being buried on its own. It's not extremely old, I can see that, but I can't tell much beyond that. I can get it tested. They'd be able to tell exactly how old it is.'

She was right, he should have gone to the police straight away. Something had held him back. Perhaps it was fear of what the truth might be.

'If it proves interesting, you must tell me where it came from, so that we can excavate the area properly. I know you might be reluctant if you're doing something with the ground, but that's the deal okay?' She looked at him warmly.

'Fair enough,' he said.

'I'm Melanie. Melanie Russell. We're from Edinburgh University.'

'Yes, I know where you're from. I read it in the paper. I'm Iain. Iain Martin.'

'If you leave me your details, I'll let you know as soon as I do. Come with me to the car.'

He followed her back up the sand and onto the grass where a number of vehicles were parked.

'The paper said this was Iron Age or something,' he said.

'Yes. There was an arrowhead found and some

preliminary excavation suggested there might be more, a settlement even, like Skara Brae in Orkney.' She talked enthusiastically. 'I'm not sure it's anything like that, but we've found some interesting items.'

'I'm sure there's a lot more hidden on this island.'

'Oh yes. Of course the islands were important connections on the sea routes. I love coming here. There's so much history, so much of it untouched.'

She opened the boot of a small saloon car and placed the bone carefully inside, then took a notebook from a leather satchel on the driver seat and took down his phone number.

'I'm sorry if I seemed a bit severe,' she said. 'I'm probably being over sensitive, but you'll keep yourself right if you get the authorities to investigate it, however much of a complication it might be.'

'I just thought it might be really old and I'd have looked a mug calling in the police.'

She laughed and Iain thought that severe was one thing she didn't seem to be.

Soon after, he was back on the road home, trying to convince himself that he had done the right thing. What was there to fear? He had done nothing wrong, so why was he so uneasy? As he rounded a bend he had to hit the brakes hard to avoid a sheep that was standing nonchalantly in the middle of the road. Gravel scraped and scratched beneath his tyres as the car pulled towards the ditch at the side of the road. He tugged at the steering wheel and finally stopped askew, but still on the road.

The sheep walked casually away. What was it with sheep? If he had been walking towards it, it would have kept a wary eye on him and more than likely run off on its spindly legs, but half a ton and more of roaring steel bearing down at speed seemed to cause it no great concern. It was remarkable how sheep would lie contentedly by the roadside, chewing away on grass, and barely glance at the wheels flashing past within mere feet of their heads. Years of working with his father's sheep had convinced him that they were stupid creatures, but their silliness sometimes came across as an almost admirable insouciance.

He had been driving too fast, there was so much on his mind. A little further up the road was a tearoom. He pulled in, bought a mug of tea and a scone and sat looking out of the window, up at a small waterfall pouring out of the moor.

There was nothing to be gained from not confronting his concerns. Quite simply, had he uncovered Rob's remains? His disquiet had crystallised. No skirting around his foreboding, avoiding thinking about it. That is what was gnawing at him. The idea seemed ridiculous, but what else could Catriona have meant? If Rob hadn't died in the way that people thought, then what had happened?

This was how he tackled anything uncomfortable, stripping away fears and uncertainties and examining the bare facts. The only reasons for him having such notions were Catriona's dramatic revelation and perhaps Neilie's manner, especially his touchiness over his plans for the old house.

Yet he had been on the shore himself that ghastly night. He had seen Neilie, the boat, the storm, everything. Did he not believe his own eyes?

The more he considered his suspicions, the more preposterous they seemed. His mood settled. When the tensions had eased, he would laugh with them about it. Whatever Catriona had been meaning, nobody knew exactly how Rob had died, apart from the fact that he had gone overboard in a storm and never been recovered. The details of his last, desperate moments were too troubling to consider.

The drive back home was more relaxed and he enjoyed steering unhurriedly around the blind bends and sweeping curves. As he returned to the junction with the main artery route of the island, he told himself yet again that he must make a greater effort to see more of the hills and sands of Uig.

With a crush of fish flesh between his fingers, Iain swept up the remains of the food on his plate. It was the best way to eat such a meal, but he could only ever do it at his mother's. Yvonne had thought it uncouth.

'That was great, Mam.'

'Are you thinking of going out tonight?'

'Just for a while.'

The day had turned leaden, ocean and sky the same drab grey. The wind was persistent and robust. He wanted to get to the house before the rain set in.

He walked up the croft, the long, wild grass reaching up to his knees. How had anyone managed to wrench survival from this unyielding earth? It was a wonder that many more hadn't grasped the opportunity to emigrate to more forgiving lands. But something bound people here, the same power that had drawn him home. Was it the splendour of the landscape? Or was it the pull of the past through the blood in their veins? However fragile the life here, this land was at the very core of who they were.

Iain climbed over the fence at the top of the croft and turned towards the sea, following the old tractor trail to the peat banks. Walking on the moor disturbed no one, apart from the occasional rabbit darting in a flash of bobtail, or the birds that chirped warnings of intrusion.

The tent was still there. Iain stood next to it and called Peter's name, but again there was no response. Both curious and concerned, he knelt down and unzipped the tent, saying Peter's name all the time. It was empty and the few possessions there were scattered rather untidily. A sleeping bag, a rucksack, a book, a large stainless steel flask and a small stove had been left where they were last used. It smelt stale, but there was no sign of anything out of order.

Iain took his usual seat on the wall of the house, but facing towards the interior, rather than the sea. His eyes drifted over the floor from the tarpaulin to the lower wall and back again. He'd barely started and there was still so much to do, but he'd stopped when he uncovered the bones.

A chilling thought hit him. What made him so sure that there was only one body there? What if the skeleton was not alone?

Chapter Nine

'ARE YOU LIVING here already?'

Iain looked sharply across the walls in the direction of the voice. Neilie was approaching, a spade slung over his shoulder.

'You're never away from the place.'

'What are you doing?' Iain asked, walking round the wall towards him.

'You're talking to me then?' Neilie said, stopping short of the entrance.

'Why wouldn't I be?'

'I was out of order last night. I can't remember much to be honest, but Cat's giving me the silent treatment, so I must have done something wrong.'

'You were drunk. We've all been there.'

'What was I saying?'

'Nothing worth listening to.'

'Well anyway, there didn't seem much point sitting with her in that sort of mood, so I thought I'd come down and do some of the hard work for you.'

'I don't fancy digging any more tonight,' said Iain.

'I'll do it,' volunteered Neilie, flourishing the spade.

'No. I want a break from it. How would you fancy going fishing?'

The idea was spontaneous, surprising Iain himself. It was an indication, perhaps, that he was settling back into the mindset that time was an easy guide, not an insistent master.

'Fishing? I like the sound of that. It's been a while. It's just the loch you're thinking of, aye?'

'Wouldn't be much time to go anywhere else. There's only a couple of hours light left at most,' said Iain looking to the sky.

'Right, let's go.'

They drove back to Neilie's house.

'We're going out,' he told Catriona. When he saw the concern in her face, he added, 'Not to the pub.'

As he went to the fridge for some cans, she threw an anxious look to Iain, who smiled and signalled with a downward movement of his open palms that everything was calm.

She came out to see them off and while Neilie went into his barn to get the fishing rods Iain asked her quietly if things were okay.

'We haven't talked much. What's this all about?'

'Just fishing. We can't keep going on the way we were.'

Neilie re-emerged with two dark green canvas bags.

'Take Ruaridh's,' he said, giving it to Iain. 'Everything will be there.'

They set off, each with a bag slung over his shoulder like a rifle and Neilie with an extra bag. Down the years it was a ritual they had done more often than either could remember. Puddles were strewn across the road's surface, but with their wellingtons on they strode through them. Less than a hundred yards down the road, they climbed a fence and were onto the moor.

Half an hour later they reached the top of a ridge beneath which was Loch Falaichte, the hidden loch. As children they had heard stories of the dangers of its forbidding waters. Iain's grandfather had whispered of a spirit that lured the unwary, the ghost of a boy who had drowned there, many, many years before, who beckoned the inquisitive and when their curiosity got the better of them, pounced, pulling them to the depths to keep him company forever.

Iain had never known for sure whether any child had ever drowned in Loch Falaichte, but he had stayed away, exactly what the old man had wanted him to do. Even as an adult, he had always been wary of these waters. The loch was set below a rim of peat banks and the sunlight barely brushed its surface. But there were fish here. Hard to get, but that was part of the challenge. Coming away from Loch Falaichte with one or two trout was as much a success as a bagful of fish from the sea.

Carefully placing their feet, they descended to the water's edge and began to work their way around the steeply rising bank. Iain slipped on the wet heather, but threw his hand against a hummock to stop himself from slithering into the water.

'You've been in the city too long, cove,' Neilie snorted with laughter and Iain couldn't stop himself from smiling.

Eventually they reached a flat rock that jutted into the water, providing a platform from which they could both cast their lines. Years before, Rob had carved his initials into it during one long night of fishing. 'RM'. They were still there, blurred slightly by lichen, but still there. A message from a life less complicated.

There was little in the way of talking as they pieced their rods together and fed the lines through the guides. Neilie opened a tobacco tin containing a collection of colourful flies.

'Take your pick,' he said.

'It's a long way from the bubble float and worms we used to use.'

'Oh, that's frowned upon now. They reckon it's too easy.'

'What one do you think?'

'It's been a while since you were out, right enough,' said Neilie looking at him in amusement. He rummaged through the box with his fingertips and picked out a fly.

'Here. Try this one. Teal, Blue and Silver. If they're biting, they'll go for it.'

Neilie gave Iain another two of the flies.

'You remember how to tie them on?'

It was fiddly, but Iain was determined to show that he hadn't forgotten the skills of his youth. By the time he finished, Neilie was ready to go.

Neilie cast first, rolling out his line, jerking the rod into the air and then flicking hard from his wrist. The line whipped through the air and landed on the water like a long, thin, worm before settling beneath the surface. Satisfied, he stooped down into a seated position and gently began to work it back with a series of gentle tugs and jiggles.

Iain had a couple of flawed casts before he too sat down, facing slightly away from Neilie, like five to one on a clock face.

Iain lit a cigarette. It had been a great way of keeping the midges from biting. These cursed creatures could send a man demented. Smoke kept them away. Before long, Iain had taken to smoking even when he wasn't fishing. It reminded him of the relaxation of fishing, he had claimed.

Soon there was the click of Neilie opening a can of Special. He passed it to Iain.

'Just like old times, eh?'

'Cheers!'

Much of the first mouthful was froth, but he relished the cool bitterness of the second.

'I doubt we'll get much tonight,' observed Iain.

'Who cares?' laughed Neilie. 'Just to be out here again. Can't beat it. I come out with the boys quite often. Something we can do together, y'know.'

Bonding with your offspring. It was a life experience Iain had missed, denied by Yvonne's career aspirations. He had been party to that choice, but his sense of regret was getting stronger and he recognised it as a huge gap in his life. The only consolation was that when they split up, there wasn't the tangled complication of a child's welfare to consider. Maybe if they'd had a child they wouldn't have split. He'd tossed these thoughts around so often. Perhaps if he didn't love the wife of the man sitting beside him, perhaps then his marriage might have stood a chance.

Iain and Neilie sat in silence, listening to the water of the loch lapping against the peat banks. The peat coloured it a deep brown. Somewhere on the moor a nesting bird called. Further away, near the village, a cow moaned to be relieved of her milk. In the village, Braggan's loom would be clacking away and a mother would be calling her children to their bath. The familiar pattern of sound was broken only by the occasional whip of a line being recast or the scoosh of a can being opened.

They got nothing, not so much as a bite, but neither was concerned. It was the peace of the fishing and their renewed ease together that made it enjoyable. What had gone before had been set aside, although Iain knew they would have to talk.

It was strange that as the night began to fall, it actually became brighter. The rain-bearing clouds had moved on and behind them was a clearer sky, allowing more sunlight through, although the sun was falling quickly.

Neilie sighed and reeled in his line, ready to grasp the

hook and fly as they swung free from the water. He slapped his hand onto the initials Rob had carved on the rock all those years before.

'Well Robbie boy, they're not biting tonight.'

Iain concentrated on securing his own line and then, as they dismantled the roads, he spoke.

'D'you think of him much?'

'Rob? Not a day passes.'

'It was sad about his mam.'

Neilie didn't respond.

'I'm the same,' continued Iain. 'Still think of him. Maybe not every day, but often. You'd have thought by now it would only be if something reminded me of him – a photograph or something. But no, sometimes he just comes into my mind.'

Neilie nodded.

'D'you remember that old Vauxhall he had? What was he, fifteen or something? And we were out on the moor road and he wanted to try the American cop routine.'

Neilie smiled at the memory.

'Was it me who was driving? It must have been. I was desperate for a shot, but I didn't really know what I was doing and I must have put too much pressure on the throttle. Remember him throwing open the door and rolling out the car? He was all set to start firing his air pistol and his foot went under the back wheel.' Iain could barely finish his story for laughing.

'It was bloody sore,' laughed Neilie, his shoulders heaving.

'And there's me whooping in the car because I'm driving, you're yelling because you rolled out no bother, and Rob's way behind, moaning because his foot went under the wheel!'

Neither man could speak for a moment. Both were sore with mirth.

'He couldn't walk for a week,' Iain roared, tears of laughter in his eyes.

'I don't know how he didn't break a bone, but there wasn't much skin left on his foot.'

They laughed themselves breathless.

'The Shawbost Dance. Remember that?' It was Neilie's turn to tell the story. 'It was that old Cortina he had then. Him and his cars.'

'The Shawbost Dance,' recalled Iain. 'You had to have those damn stamps on your hand that showed up under the ultraviolet.'

'Oh, we were well fu' that night. It was like something out of the Wild West. All those cars in the car park and they've got glasses lined up along the dashboards. When I think of it. And Rob decides he wants to move the car. 'Right a' bhalaich,' he says, slamming it into reverse and shooting back straight into Lexy's motor behind him. Lexy's in there with some girl and the two of them end up with smashed front teeth.'

Iain was making strange noises as he tried to catch his breath through his laughter.

'And Rob,' he managed to say, 'He burns his nose on his fag against the steering wheel.'

It was just like old times, bonding like brothers.

'He loved his cars, did Rob,' sighed Neilie, before another explosion of laughter burst through. 'Couldn't drive one of the damn things without a handbrake turn somewhere along the way.'

'What would he be doing now?' Iain wondered.

'The fishing,' answered Neilie with certainty. 'Can't imagine he'd have done anything else. It would have driven him mad. Sitting in an office? It just wouldn't have happened.'

The jocularity expired as they considered the life their friend never had. Iain saw the sadness in Neilie's eyes as he opened the last two beers.

'Neilie, what's this all about? The other night...'

'Can a man not have a drink?'

'Nobody's saying you can't. I certainly couldn't say it, I enjoy it as much as the next man, but there's drinking for the craic and there's drinking to forget. I reckon you're trying to forget something. Or, at least, hide from it.'

'Who's been talking? Like I didn't know.'

'Nobody. I've seen it myself. You never used to drink like that. You got plastered the night of Rob's mother's funeral.'

'So did you.'

'Not in the same way.'

Neilie stared over the loch, but made no effort to leave. He had known that this conversation would have to happen. They had looked out for each other since they were boys and friction or problems had never been allowed to fester.

'She never blamed you, you know that,' continued Iain.

'No,' responded Neilie, his head dropping.

'Nobody ever blamed you. It wasn't your fault.'

'Maybe not.'

'So why torture yourself over it?'

Neilie ran his fingertips over the initials in the rock. He inhaled deeply.

'I remember going to the house for the first time after it happened. It was the silence that got to me. She was always so chatty, y'know. Remember, Rob said that's why his old man was so quiet – because he never got the chance. But she had such a big heart. Anyway, that night, it must have been a couple of days later, before the service. It was just so quiet. His old man was sitting in his chair and she was by the stove. It was so still, so still and quiet. And I didn't know what to say. What could I say? She asks me if I was okay. She tells me that it's good to see me. She mentioned you as well. Says we weren't to be strangers and that having us in the house would make her feel as if Rob was still there somehow.'

Iain nodded. She had told him the same thing. Neilie was struggling with his emotions.

'Well, at that she starts crying and runs out of the room. So it's just me and his old man. He's looking towards the door until we can't hear her any more. I'm sitting there and he says to me, "What happened?" Well, I can't look at him. He says to me again, "What happened?" He's sitting forward in his chair staring right at me. Right through me. I tell him I don't know exactly, that it all happened so fast. And he says, "What warning did you have?" "None," I says. "It just came up like that?" he says, snapping his fingers.'

Neilie clicked his fingers just as Rob's father must have done. Iain hardly dared to breathe. He had never heard Neilie speak of this before.

'I says something about us not expecting it. He asks me how the wave hit us, says, "Was it at the stern or broadsides?" I says I wasn't sure. He asks what had we done when we first saw the storm coming. He asks me where Rob was in the boat and where was I. Just questions all the time. "Did you hear him call?" he says. I'm shaking now. "Neilie, did you hear him call? Did you hear my boy call to you?" "Oh, God!" I says.'

Now the tears came, coursing over his cheeks into the

corners of his mouth. His hands trembled and he clasped them to keep them steady.

'"Did you hear my boy call?" I mean, how are you supposed to answer that?' Neilie looked despairingly at Iain, who shook his head sympathetically.

'Anyway,' he sniffed deeply, regaining some composure, 'Rob's mam comes back in and he's sat back in his seat, but he doesn't take his eyes off me. She apologises for getting upset and I say I'd best be off. She sees me to the door and as I'm walking away she tells me again not to be a stranger.'

Neilie twisted to take a swig from the can at his side. Iain took out his cigarettes and gave him one. As he lit them, Iain said, 'He probably didn't mean to be so harsh. Some people want to know everything about the final moments. Helps them grieve.'

Neilie scraped a loose flake of tobacco from his mouth using the third finger of the hand holding the cigarette.

'No, it wasn't that.'

'Rob's old man took it hard. He died not long after. Couple of years or so.'

'No, you don't understand. He knew.'

'Knew what?'

'That I wasn't there.'

Iain frowned in confusion.

'I wasn't in the boat. I was never there.'

Chapter Ten

THE TWO LIFELONG friends sat on the rock of the hidden loch as one unburdened himself of a secret he had borne for half his life, fearful of what its revelation might bring.

Neilie and Rob had set out from Iain's house intending to go fishing. Earlier Rob had sailed the boat from its usual moorings at the mouth of the river, round the headland and anchored it in the bay. It was a trip Neilie had been looking forward to and when Iain refused to go, he had bad-mouthed him.

'I was calling you for everything, but Rob wasn't having it. Things calm down and then I finally tell him that Catriona and I are going out together. Well, you know Rob, usually so laid back. Boy, he tore into me! Said I was being a fool. It just wasn't Rob at all. He was cursing me. Said I was messing things up. That Catriona was your girl.'

Iain struggled to keep the tears from his eyes when he learned how Rob had stood up for him.

'You've got to understand,' continued Neilie, 'Catriona was everything to me then. She still is. She made me more than I could be on my own. The two of you had split up and you had all these girls in the city if you wanted. I didn't see that I was doing anything wrong. I got riled at Rob and said Cat wasn't tied to anyone and that it was nothing to do with him, unless he had his eye on her. That's how it went until I told him he could forget the fishing, and I walked away.'

'And he carried on?'

'Yes. Last I saw he was heading down to the shore. I started walking up onto the cliffs. I was raging. I needed to clear my head. Maybe I thought he might come back up behind me or just go off home. But he was in a strange mood, the way he turned on me. That wasn't like him. When I was up on the cliffs I tried to spot him. I could see most of the bay, but not him. Maybe he was keeping tight to the shoreline. I couldn't see him, anyway. I'm sitting there on the cliff going over things, when I feel the wind blowing on my face. Not the usual. Really strong. Just like that, all of a sudden. I don't know where that storm came from, I've never seen the likes of it. There's no sign of Rob, so I run down to the shore. That took maybe fifteen minutes. When I get there, there's nothing to see. Nothing. The waves were coming way up the shore and it was so dark I could hardly see the headland. I was getting frantic, and then I saw the boat. It was just a glimpse, but I saw it and, oh, the relief. Then it reappeared and then again, getting closer to the shore. I'm looking around for a rope. A couple of minutes later the boat gets thrown onto the shore and he's not on it. Rob's not there, he's gone. Well, you know the rest,' he said with a curt wave of his hand.

Iain absorbed all this for a few moments.

'I don't understand. Why did you say you were in the boat with him?'

'I didn't.'

Neilie spat into the loch, the white globule immediately breaking up in the dark waters.

'I always thought you were in the boat. I saw you myself. You were drenched. Shaking.'

'Anyone on the shore that night would have been soaked. No, I never said. Dan did. I ran up to his house for help and he must have assumed I was in the boat. It was only later when people were asking me what had happened and how had I managed to stay on board that I realised. I'd probably been too shocked before. By then it was too late. Everyone was saying that I'd been on the boat and it would have seemed pretty strange if I suddenly said I wasn't. And anyway, it didn't change anything. Rob was gone.'

'Did you ever actually see him in the boat?' asked Iain, beginning to make connections in his mind.

'No. But that's where he was headed.'

The darkness was spreading over the nooks and knolls, enclosing them in the night. Both sensed it was time to go and gathered up their bags. Neilie threw his empty can into the loch. It was lost in the gloom, but they could hear it slap onto the water. It would float there until it filled and sank. That would be long enough. This was their land and they were so used to it that at times they could be careless of it.

They worked their way back the way they had come. Iain stumbled once or twice on a heather root, but they had no real difficulty. The rocks took on a luminosity in the moonlight and they could navigate by them.

As they trudged along, Iain asked, 'How do you think he knew? Rob's dad? How could he know?'

'I've no idea. He was a seaman. Maybe he could just tell. He didn't ask me again. He never had much of a chance to, I hardly ever saw him. I'd only call when I knew he was out. Then he died himself. He was all twisted up because they'd had a big blowup that night, him and Rob. That's why Rob wanted to go out on the boat so sudden. Remember his old man used to say there was no future in the fishing and that Rob should get out and do something else.'

'He was always saying that,' agreed Iain.

'Rob told me they'd had a shouting match. Maybe that's why he was so sharp with me later, I don't know. I'll never know.'

'Did she know, Rob's mam?'

'If she did, she never said. That's what got me so hard when she died. She was just so good. Despite all that happened, she was the same to me. If she knew, she never cast it up to me and if she didn't know, she never made me feel like she resented me surviving.'

They'd reached the fence next to the road. After the yielding tread on the moor, their first footsteps on the tarmac jarred. The light from Neilie's house fell just short of them.

'Who else knows?' asked Iain. 'Cat?'

'She does now, but she didn't for long enough. Other than that nobody.'

'Christ Neilie, that's a hell of a thing to keep to yourself all this time.'

'Who was I going to tell? You? What would you think of me? What good would it do?'

Catriona's anxious face appeared at the front window and when she saw them coming up the drive together she went through to meet them at the back door.

'I was beginning to get worried,' she said, looking quickly from one to the other, checking for signs of tension between them. When she saw that there wasn't, she visibly relaxed.

'They weren't for biting,' said Neilie, 'So, nothing for supper.'

'Are you for staying?' she asked Iain.

How he would have liked to, if only to spend more time in Catriona's company. But he didn't think it would be right.

'Thanks, but I'll get on up the road.'

'You and your mother must come for dinner tomorrow. No arguments, okay. Tomorrow. After church.'

Neilie went to return the fishing rods to the barn. As soon as he disappeared through the door, Catriona asked, 'Is everything okay?'

'Yes, fine. Nothing to worry about. We had a good talk.'

What a strain she seemed to be living under. Iain was painfully aware it was not his place to protect her, so he said good night and left. Walking away from her was an effort. Her pull on him seemed to be ever stronger. Was it because he saw a weakness in her marriage? Was he playing up to the role of the one she could turn to for comfort and solace? Not deliberately, he tried to convince himself, but deep down did he want their relationship to disintegrate?

Catriona's voice carried through the darkness. The words she was saying to her husband were indistinct, but it was her speaking and it hit him so forcibly that he wanted her to be speaking to him. Could he really be so callous as to come between two people who were his friends? Neilie had trusted him enough to expose his soul to him. How could he betray that? What arrogance, to assume that he could come between them. And how contemptible even to think of it. This was a struggle between heart and head and it disturbed him deeply. Walking away was all that he could do.

The next day was Sunday, the Sabbath. The Bible said, 'Six days shalt thou labour and do all thy work. But the seventh day is the Sabbath of the Lord thy God: in it thou shalt not do any work, thou, nor thy son…' Iain had learned that as a child at Sunday School and his father had quoted it often when he and Kenny had argued against the restrictions imposed.

'It's there in Exodus. Plain as day,' he would say and then run his finger further down the passage. '"Six days thou shalt do thy work, and on the seventh thou shalt rest." That's what it says boy. You either believe what the Bible says or you don't. You don't pick the bits that suit you.'

The Lord had rested on the seventh day and it was to His praise that all activity on the Sabbath must be focused. Nowhere was this more rigidly observed than here on the island. The family went to church twice, morning and evening, to read God's Word, to sing psalms of praise and pray forgiveness and thanks. There must be no distraction; no television or radio, no playing outside, no newspapers. To the outsider, it was as if the island closed down. No shops or pubs or works were open, no ferries sailed, no aircraft flew.

How Iain had kicked against the restrictions as he grew up. It was torture, of a kind. The football sitting in the barn took on temptation beyond all reason. Just knowing it was there and that he couldn't kick it agitated him to distraction. He had almost choked with frustration at missing some of the major World Cup games televised live on a Sunday. With teenage years came cockiness and some Sundays he and Kenny used to disappear to the barn with their transistor radio and listen to the pop stations or kick the ball around. Never for too long, though, because that would lead to discovery. He had long believed that his parents must have suspected and chosen to ignore it, but now he wasn't so sure. They had instilled in their children the importance of their faith and simply trusted them not to abuse it.

The one activity permissible was walking. Long rambles across the moor began as nothing more than an escape from the confines of the Sabbath, but developed into a routine that he missed if the weather was particularly unpleasant.

Over the years, his attitude to the Sabbatarianism changed. He grew to enjoy the peace of a Sunday, to appreciate the guarantee of rest. This was his state of mind now. It was Sunday, so there could be no digging at the house. After a troubled night during which all that had seemed certain was in disarray, it would be no bad thing to have a period of contemplation.

During his years on the mainland he had drifted away from the church through idleness, distraction and disaffection. But at times of real crisis, he had turned to it for strength, comfort and understanding. The first time had been when Rob died and then, later, when his own father passed away. He had needed more than the physical bond of holding onto someone in those dark times, Catriona in the first instance, Yvonne in the second. He had felt spiritually lost and had anchored himself to the church until his fears subsided and he found himself set adrift again.

For his mother, the church was the great constant throughout her life, the Bible the last thing she read every night. That faith gave her a spiritual peace that Iain craved, but could not attain. He had long struggled with the concept of God, Lord of all. It had been the theme of many a philosophical discussion in his days as a student, when his peers exercised their minds on the question of being. Their views ranged from the sceptical to the downright dismissive. He had considered himself enlightened. His parents and those of faith believed what they had been taught without question. His education had encouraged him to question, dissect and analyse and his mind was the sharper for it.

Or was it? That was the doubt that troubled him now. Those old folk whose beliefs he had deemed worthy of scorn lived on the very margins of existence and they had close experience of death's clammy hand from a young age. Their faith was real and enduring. The island men who had seen the slaughter of the battlefields, who had been so brutally exposed to man's inhumanity to man, those old fellows had been the stalwarts of the church in which he'd been raised. Why be so sure that they were wrong? The uncertainty grew the older he became.

That was why he was in church with his mother on the Sunday morning. And for the simple fact that it pleased her.

It was the usual service; the unaccompanied psalm singing, standing for the prayers and the sermon that he could never follow. So much remained unchanged from his childhood: the routine, the hats on grey heads and the sighing of the cailleachs sitting down during the long opening prayer. He smiled silently as he recalled betting sweets with Kenny on which of the women would be the first to succumb.

Ah, the protocol of the sweets! Never to be consumed during the opening rituals of the service, but only after the minister had read from the Bible and was preparing to preach. Then the wrappers would rustle as the mint humbugs, butterscotch or toffee caramels were surreptitiously slipped into their mouths.

Whatever confusion loitered in his mind about the meaning of the church's message, the warmth of the people who filled the pews was never in doubt.

At the conclusion of the service they gathered outside and exchanged greetings and gossip. A number of the elderly folk of the district approached him and inquired of his welfare.

'Iain, a' ghraidh, it's so good to see you. How are you keeping? You're back to stay, I hear.'

The companionship that brought many so faithfully to the church was palpable.

Eventually, Mary approached him with Agnes. Would he mind running her home? Iain knew Agnes as a woman of independent spirit, but she was getting on in years and the walk to the church must be an increasing struggle for her. The two women talked incessantly in the back of the car during the short journey.

If it wasn't for the dinner invitation, Mary would have quite happily gone in for a cup of tea and the chat would have lasted through the afternoon. Dinner was to be early because, although Neilie and Catriona weren't regular churchgoers, they knew that Mary would want to return for the evening service.

Back at home, Mary busied herself getting ready. Church clothes were for church and she must change for dinner. Iain sat watching her searching through the cupboard in the kitchen.

'I don't think I've got anything for the children.'

'Ma, they're teenagers. They don't need sweets. Anyway, there's not much chance of you seeing them. They'll be off somewhere.'

Catriona's first pregnancy had been a time of confused emotions for Iain. It meant acceptance that she was bound to someone else and a realisation that time was passing. The child carried his father's name, but his middle name was in tribute to Rob. Neilie had opposed the idea: 'He's got to have his own identity,' he'd said. But Catriona had insisted. A second son, Ruaridh, followed two years later. By then Iain was immersed in building his life with Yvonne.

When Mary was prepared, Iain drove the short distance

to Neilie and Catriona's house. The initial chat was all about the news from the church and around the village. Somebody had broken a leg, another was being flown to hospital on the mainland, someone's son had a prestigious new job and how the weavers were suffering from a dearth of orders.

'How are you keeping, yourself?' Catriona asked Mary.

'I'm fine, fine,' she replied openly.

'She had us worried there for a while,' Catriona said to Iain. 'The doctor kept wanting to see her.'

'And how's your mother?' Mary interrupted, 'I didn't see her at the church this morning.'

Neilie appeared from upstairs and his voice filled the room.

'Hi, folks. What's doing?'

Mary's warmth towards him was instant. Iain could see it. This was a man who was good to her, whom she trusted.

'Did he tell you about the fishing last night?' Neilie asked her cheerily.

'No?'

'Not a thing, not even a bite. I think he's lost his touch. It's all that soft living in Glasgow. You want a fish there, you get it battered with chips.'

'I didn't see you have any more success,' laughed Iain.

'You scared them away,' retorted Neilie. 'What did he get for supper last night, eh? No fresh trout that's for sure. And me neither.'

Catriona called them through. The two boys appeared and made their dutiful hellos. Iain couldn't help but notice how like his mother the younger son was.

Dinner was traditional fare: broth, roasted meat with potatoes and root vegetables, followed by dessert. Neilie muttered grace for Mary's benefit.

'So how's the house coming on?' Catriona asked as they raised their heads again.

'Oh, you hear nothing,' said Mary. 'Away all day, then it's off to Uig, then fishing.'

'Uig?' asked Neilie, 'What took you over there?'

'Some historian, or what is it? Archaeologist,' Mary answered for him.

'Archaeologist?' asked Catriona in surprise.

'I just wanted to ask them some questions about the old houses.'

'Yes, but you said you'd found something,' said Mary.

'Oh?' Catriona and Neilie were looking at him.

'It was nothing really.'

They waited expectantly.

'I'm not really sure what it was. That's why I went to see them.'

'What was it like?' Catriona pressed.

'It's difficult to say,' stammered Iain, his mind grasping for anything convincing. 'It was an iron thing, a handle or something.'

'A handle? I told him he should've shown it to me. It likely came from a pot. But, oh no, nothing would do but he had to go all the way over to Uig to ask someone who's probably only ever seen a picture of it in a book.'

'And did they know, could they tell you?'

'No, they have to get it analysed.'

'Analysed?' said Catriona in surprise. 'You'd think they'd know whether it was a handle or not.'

'Well yes, but they couldn't tell the age right away.'

'Where did you find it?' It was Neilie's voice.

'Under the floor.'

'Aye, but whereabouts?' Neilie persisted. 'Where in the house?'

'By the fireplace.' Iain was uncomfortable.

'By the fireplace?'

'Yes.'

'You found a pot handle under the floor next to the fireplace and you have to get an archaeologist to tell you what it is?' There was a note of incredulity in Neilie's voice.

'No, Neilie,' Catriona defended him. 'He said he wanted to find out how old it was.'

'What, like Iron Age or something?' laughed Neilie. 'You find a pot handle next to a fireplace in a house that was built maybe a hundred and fifty years ago and you can't imagine how old it is. Figure it out.'

Mary was laughing with him. Iain blushed deep red.

'Hey, boy,' continued Neilie, 'Maybe you'll find some false teeth where the beds were and think they're Stone Age.'

He could have retaliated, but looking at the smiling faces around him, he knew he'd rather be the butt of their gentle ridicule than have the truth coming out just now.

Mary helped clear up the soup plates, while Catriona brought through the ready-carved meat.

'Did you kill a beast?' asked Iain.

'Two,' said Neilie. 'Called Mark and Spencer.'

'Ah. From the freezer then?'

Everyone helped themselves from the hot dishes before the conversation continued. It was Neilie who began.

'Seriously, Iain, about the house. Have you thought this through? Have you got planning permission for anything? Have you even planned out what you're doing?'

'Not really. I'm just seeing how it goes.'

'You'll save yourself a lot of trouble if you get it sorted now. I mean, you're talking about clearing the floor, but you'd be better taking down the walls and starting from scratch. You can't build that back up again. You're probably in breach of all sorts of regulations.'

'Pull the walls down?'

'I think you'll have to. You can't just put a roof over it and say, "This is now my house and I'm staying here." They'll not let you away with it.'

'Who won't?'

'The usual. The bureaucrats, the pen pushers. If you don't have a bit of paper for this or that, they come down on you. They have to. It's the only way they can justify their existence. We come up against it all the time.'

'Well I suppose there has to be some control,' threw in Catriona. 'You can't just have people building all over the place. I'm not saying that's what you're doing, but there has to be some sort of regulation.'

'Well, they make the most of it, is all I'm saying. The point is that if you build the existing house up and start living in it, I guarantee they'll come looking for you.'

'But pulling down the walls would defeat the whole purpose. I told you that there was something about living within the walls my ancestors built,' protested Iain.

'That's for the toffs,' said Neilie dismissively. 'They can live in their big castles for generations. The rest of us can't get away with that. We're hassled, we were then and we are now.'

'Oh don't start on the politics, Neilie,' said Catriona, irritation in her voice.

'All I'm saying is, I don't think you can do it the way you're saying. If you want to build the walls up again, there are ways to do it. As it is, you've got no insulation, nothing.'

Iain played with the food on his plate.

'That's why I said to you at the start that I'd clear the

site for you and then you can do it properly.'

Iain didn't say anything.

'If I come across any more pot handles, I'll be sure to give them to you.'

The laughter trickled round the table again and the conversation moved on. Mary excused herself and went to the bathroom.

'How is she?' Neilie asked quietly.

'I thought she was fine. Maybe a bit forgetful, but she said nothing to me about being at the doctor.'

'She never said what it was for, you know your mother. It couldn't have been anything if she never said.'

'She's never at the doctor's.'

'She'd have said if it was anything to worry about.' Catriona regretted making any mention of it. Mary's return put an end to the subject. Then the phone rang. Neilie pulled himself out of his chair and went through to the hall to answer it. He was back after a couple of monosyllabic grunts.

'It's my mother. One of the cows has got out onto the road. I'll need to go.'

'I'll come with you,' offered Iain, already half way out of his chair.

'It's alright. The boys can come.' He gestured to his sons. 'C'mon.'

The door slammed, followed quickly by a car engine coughing to life and then the scrunch of tyres on the driveway.

'I'll get the dishes done,' said Catriona, carrying some plates into the kitchen. She declined Mary's offer to help, insisting she have a seat through in the living-room.

'Let me help,' offered Iain.

Catriona turned on the hot water tap and squirted

washing up liquid into the basin.

'Stay in there with your mam.'

'I need to speak to you,' said Iain.

She threw a dish towel to him and pulled on a pair of rubber gloves without catching his eye. Iain walked over to stand beside her at the sink. He could smell her scent, its softness beneath the citrus of the dish water. He wanted to touch her, so wanted to touch her, even just to brush her hand with his. She kept her eyes on the plate she was scouring.

'He told me last night,' began Iain. 'He told me everything about the night Rob died.'

'And what was "everything"?' She looked sharply at him.

'About how they argued. That he didn't go on the boat with him and that Rob carried on on his own. How the storm blew up and he couldn't do anything. He feels so bad about it. All those years he's carried that.'

'I know. He told me last year, when Rob's mother died. He got drunk and started crying and it all came out then.'

For a while, the only sound was the sloshing of the water in the basin and the clatter of the crockery being placed on the draining board.

'D'you know what the row was about?'

Catriona didn't reply.

'Do you know?'

'He never said.'

'It was about you.'

'Me?'

'They argued about you. He must have told you that.'

'No. He didn't.'

Suddenly she whirled round, a blaze in her eyes.

'And why are you telling me? What difference does it

make what they argued about?'

Iain was startled. 'In case you were blaming yourself for anything...'

'Why would I do that?'

'It doesn't matter. I just thought... We all carry some guilt about it. I feel bad that I didn't go with them. I thought maybe you knew what they'd argued about and maybe you were trying to hide it. That's all. I was just going to say that Rob was already fired up about something. He'd had a row with his old man. Nobody was to blame.'

'Well, that's good of you to say so,' Catriona said sarcastically.

'I don't understand. What's the problem? This isn't like you.'

Catriona started crying suddenly.

'Rob was in a mood because of me,' she said, her hands unable to wipe her eyes because of the suds on the rubber gloves she was wearing. 'It was nothing to do with his father.'

Iain stepped back. Catriona continued, her voice straining to keep control of her voice.

'I told him that Neilie and I were going out together. He got angry with me. Asked me, what was I playing at? He said that you were the one for me and that I knew it. But Iain, Neilie was so good to me. It was when my father died, remember?'

Iain nodded. She sniffed and tried to wipe her eyes on the sleeves of her blouse.

'He said I was going to cause a rift between you and Neilie and that I would just make Neilie unhappy. I left him that night resenting what he'd said. Maybe I even hated him. That was the last time I saw him.'

Iain put an arm on her shoulder and lightly pressed the

dish towel against her face to absorb her tears. He moved his arm round her back and pulled her closer to him. He breathed in to ask her the question when the back door clicked. Neilie stepped into the kitchen, registering the scene before him with barely a flicker. Iain pulled away from Catriona a shade more urgently than necessary. She turned abruptly back to the sink.

'The damn thing went back into the field on its own. It was already there when we arrived so we just turned straight back. It must have realised it was Sunday and there was nothing happening anywhere.'

Neilie was acting as if there was nothing amiss.

Mary came through from the living-room and looked to Iain.

'If we're going to the church maybe we'd better think about getting ready.'

It was a relief to have something to do.

Moments later they were leaving the house with Neilie and a red-eyed Catriona smiling at the door.

'I've been thinking,' said Neilie to Iain. 'After last night we need to get you out on a boat. Get some proper fishing done. You and me together, like the old times. What do you say?'

Chapter Eleven

THE FOLLOWING MORNING Iain started digging next to where he had uncovered the skeleton and worked steadily down the length of the house in a zigzag pattern. Progress was slow; being too vigorous with the spade might cause damage to whatever might be there. The days of inactivity told, and his muscles quickly strained and knotted, forcing him to take frequent breaks.

The sun failed wanly to break through the drift of clouds that carried occasional heavy showers. Rain and perspiration intermingled uncomfortably, but Iain stuck to his task.

The job was different now. This wasn't so much about reconnecting with the past as an investigation into the fate of the person whose remains he had stumbled across. It filled him with agitation to think he was being drawn ever closer to a conclusion that could tear apart so much that he valued.

The soil seemed unwilling to give up its secrets. Stones impeded the thrust of his spade and roots stubbornly bound the earth together. After two hours, a glint of white made his heart jump. He stood back to compose himself and wipe away a bead of sweat from the corner of his eye. He rocked between relief and alarm. Another skeleton would open a whole new dimension and put paid to his current suspicions. The dark scenario skulking in his mind involved only the one body. But then, there would still be the uneasy issue of what he had exposed. How many bodies might there be and why were they here? Who had buried them?

Using a trowel, he carefully excavated around it. It was bone, of that there was no question. The more he scraped the more he uncovered. The dirt seemed to fill every crevice. The tip of the trowel encountered less resistance and he saw that it was an eye socket. There was something about the angle of it that disconcerted him, then he saw a bulge at the top of the skull, and then he recognised the ribbed texture of a horn. It was a sheep that had died and decomposed a long time ago. In all likelihood it had been walking along the top of the wall and fallen. With the ferocity of frustration, Iain yanked the skull from the ground and threw it against the wall, where it clattered dully.

He was back to where he'd started that morning, riddled with apprehension and misgivings.

He stomped out through the doorway, suppressing his aggravation by holding his breath. It took all his self-control not to kick Peter's tent. Why was it still there? Where was he? Most backpackers remained for a single night, maybe two, and then they were away. But of Peter there was no sign. Should he be concerned about that? Had the man hurt himself, or was there something more irregular going on? He looked in the tent and everything was exactly as it had been before. Peter evidently hadn't returned.

Iain was aware that things were getting on top of him. Common sense told him he could not do all this on his own. Neilie's invitation the previous night had chilled him. It had seemed innocuous enough and Catriona and his mother had encouraged him to go on the next fishing trip, but Iain was consumed by suspicion. Through another fitful night, he had rebuked himself for being irrational. Neilie was his friend, always had been. He knew him as well as his own brother, had seen him in myriad situations and there was no badness in him.

It was the invitation to go out fishing that had shaken Iain, especially after Neilie's restrained reaction to seeing his wife and best friend in what was, by any standards, a compromising position. Until then, Iain had been convinced by Neilie's account of events on the night of Rob's death. But a man who could so effectively conceal any reaction to what must have seemed a devastating betrayal, what more could he be capable of?

Or was he being hysterical, seeing his friend in such a light? It would be better for everyone, himself especially, if he took a step back and let someone else establish the truth.

Without even returning to the house, he walked away home again. There were no other remains to be found, of that he was certain now. He couldn't bear the thought that he had found Rob's body. Tormented by visions matching the smiling lad with the grinning skeleton, he told himself, this must end.

'What's wrong?' asked his mother as he pulled off his wellingtons at the door, his face set grim.

'Nothing, just a slight concern,' he replied flatly, hanging his jacket at the back of the door and walking through to wash his hands in the kitchen.

'About what?'

'That German lad in the tent. There's been no sign of him for a few days. He hasn't been back. I don't like it, so I'd better get the police to check.'

'Oh dear, that doesn't sound so good. Do you think he's fallen?'

'That's what worries me. Maybe they'll get the coastguard involved. They've got their helicopters and everything. It might be nothing, but it's best to make sure.'

'I'll get the number for you. He's a nice boy, the constable. Alan, that's his name. His wife is so nice and they have two lovely daughters. It must be three years since he came.'

This information was relayed as Mary went through to the living-room for the phone directory.

'Three years? He'll be moving on soon I suppose.'

'I think he'll still have another couple of years or so. They don't let them stay on for long, mind you. Now let me see. Yes here it is.'

Mary read out the number and Iain dialled. He left a message with the policeman's wife. As he sat down, his mother put on the kettle.

'Mam,' he began, 'This might sound daft, but have you ever heard of bodies being buried in houses?'

'What?' she asked over the gurgle of the water filling the kettle.

'Bodies. You never heard of people burying bodies in houses?'

'*In* houses? Goodness me no. Where did you get that idea? No. They sometimes used to take them by boat over to Bernera. But that was a long time ago. Now it's the cemetery. In a house? How could anyone get a Christian burial in a house?'

It was no more than he expected, but it removed the possibility of his missing something obvious. As the kettle boiled, Mary asked again, 'Where did you get that idea?'

'It's nothing. I just wondered.'

She looked at him as she poured the boiling water into a teapot.

'Did you find something in the road?'

'Just a bone. I'm sure it's animal, but you never know.'

'I wonder what goes through your mind at times. Do you think the folk here were savages?'

'Forget it, Mam. I just wondered.'

'Bodies in houses, indeed!' Mary was indignant. 'Have you ever heard the likes?'

Iain sank down into the chair, his shoulders hunched up. He was tired and weary. This wasn't how it was supposed to be. Skeletons, missing persons and him at the centre of it all. His mother was still looking strangely at him when she brought him his tea.

'It was nothing, Mam,' he said quite deliberately. 'Just something I was wondering about.'

The phone rang.

'I'll get it. It'll be for me,' said Iain.

It was, too. The policeman had got his message and Iain told him of his concerns. Fifteen minutes later, a white, mark II Ford Escort with the constabulary insignia along its flanks, pulled up outside.

Alan Gibson, square of jaw and shoulder, looked quite the figure of authority in his uniform, even without the hat he'd left in the car. He introduced himself to Iain and saw his mother behind him.

'Hello, Mrs Martin. How are you keeping today?' His accent was of the mainland's central belt.

'Fine thank you, Alan.'

Mary's voice took the more formal tone she always used when she spoke to a figure of authority.

'And how's your family?' she asked politely.

'Oh fine, thanks. Getting big.'

'Would you like a cup of tea?'

'No thanks. I'd better get down to the shore with your son and see what this is all about.'

He was already walking back round to the driver's door.

Iain got into the passenger side a little uncertainly, wondering if perhaps he should be going into the back seat. The policeman registered his hesitation.

'It's only the drunks go in the back,' he laughed. 'Don't want them messing the front.'

Iain warmed to him straight away. There was barely time to buckle his seat-belt before the car shot away in a spray of stones. This was a man who enjoyed speed and the insignia on his car allowed him to indulge it. He drove with assurance, but faster than Iain thought safe. They covered the quarter of a mile to the shore in no time.

The policeman got out his hat and placed it carefully on his head, shifting it back and forth a couple of times to set it. He waited for Iain to come alongside him and then they strode up towards the old house. The tent was clearly visible from the road.

'This is it, I take it?' asked Gibson.

'Yes,' answered Iain. 'That's the way it's been for the past three days. No sign of anything.'

Gibson walked round the tent, bending forward once or twice to check something that caught his eye.

'And you've looked inside?'

'Yes, twice. He hasn't been back. That's why I'm concerned.'

'Aye I suppose.'

Gibson pulled open the zip and knelt inside for a few moments, only the distinctive soles of his Dr Marten shoes protruding through the door.

'There's nothing in there to tell us anything. And you were speaking to him, you said?'

'Yes, the other night. He seemed fine.'

'What did you say his name was? Peter?'

Iain nodded.

'And he was talking alright?'

'Yes, he seemed fine. Said he'd been here before and that it was a special place for him and his girlfriend, but that she'd died. I mean, he wasn't exactly skipping about when he told me that, but he wasn't breaking down either. It just came out in the conversation. If he was depressed or anything, it didn't show.'

'You're down here every day?'

'Most days.'

'Well, if he reappears, or even if it's just that the tent has disappeared, let me know. I'll get onto the coastguard and see if they can do a helicopter sweep down the coast in case he's fallen. That's far quicker than trying to do anything on foot and they're more likely to spot him if he's close to the cliffs. Maybe he's just wandered off and met someone somewhere else. We'll see if he turns up over the next day or two. I'm not sure that there's much else we can do for now.'

Gibson scribbled something in his notebook and then replaced it in his breast pocket and buttoned it up with one hand.

'So you're the one redeveloping the old blackhouse, are you?' he went on breezily.

'That was the original idea, but I don't know.'

'Having your doubts? I'm not surprised. That'll be a hell of a job. Why d'you want to stay down here, anyway? That sea's frightening in the winter. The first time I saw these huge waves throwing chunks of rock up to the top of the shoreline, I don't mind telling you, I was scared. I'm still not too comfortable with it, to be honest.'

The policeman began to walk round the house.

'Will you have to take this wall down?'

'I hadn't intended too, but I'm thinking I will probably

have to,' said Iain.

'It's some job you've set yourself.'

Gibson was round the back of the house.

'Have you done much inside?' he called over the wall.

'That's where I've been most of the time, just digging up the floor.'

The policeman rejoined him at the door.

'May I?' he indicated towards the opening.

'Of course.'

This was the moment of decision. How easy it would be to unload his suspicions now and pass the burden to someone else. But of course, it wouldn't go away, he would still be involved. Whatever the fall out, he could not escape. He was tangled in the net that he himself had cast. He followed Gibson into the house.

'You've been busy.'

'Yes, but I've enjoyed it. Constable...'

'Call me Alan.'

'Alan, I...'

He was interrupted by a bellowing voice.

'Has he been up to no good, Alan?'

It was Neilie, filling the house with his presence. Iain trembled.

'Neilie!' hailed the policeman. 'Just looking at this man's work. He's been hard at it.'

Neilie glanced round.

'Aye. I've told him he's making it harder than it needs to be, but he's determined. He's been finding treasures though. I'll bet he hasn't told you that. The things he's found here.'

Gibson looked at Iain with amusement.

'Pot handles!' declared Neilie. 'That's all he's come up with. Pot handles. Someone told him the old folk had hidden the family gold here.' He laughed and Gibson chuckled, shaking his head. Iain forced a smile.

'Not many would choose to do it,' said Gibson.

'There's not many daft enough.'

'Anyway, I'll have to excuse myself.' Gibson said. 'Like I said, if you see anything, let me know. I'll get onto the coastguard. Do you want a lift back up the road?'

Neilie answered for Iain. 'No, we'll walk.'

Iain felt helpless and weak. How could he fear Neilie so much?

Gibson was gone.

'What was all that about?' Neilie's voice was affable, without menace. Without menace? This was Neilie, for goodness sake.

'The tent.' Iain's throat was dry. 'There's been no movement near it for a couple of days. I thought I'd better let the police know. It's a German guy.'

'That's the thing. If these coves are on their own and they go walking up the cliffs and fall, how's anyone going to know? Remember that old fellow, years ago? Came on the bus from town. No one even knew he was here. What was it? Three days he was stuck? He was lucky to be alive.'

Iain could only nod. Neilie was pacing around, not even looking over to the fireplace.

'So are you carrying on, or what?'

'Everyone's telling me not to.'

'It makes sense. If you want to do it properly I'll help, but you'll get nowhere doing this. Think about it. Anyway, you've heard what I have to say and that's not why I came. I can get the boat on Wednesday. We'll go out a couple of miles. A few cans and some peace and quiet. C'mon, it'll be great.'

'Aye, Wednesday's fine.' Iain didn't know what else to

say. What excuse could he give that wouldn't sound ridiculous? Neilie's manner unnerved him. He seemed so casual, so relaxed.

'Right you are then.'

'Neilie. About yesterday. Me and Cat. She was upset and I was just trying to comfort her. We'd been talking about Rob.'

Neilie looked at him, unconcerned.

'I know. Don't worry. Cat told me about it later. Are you wanting a lift back home?'

Iain declined.

He needed time to think. Neilie had left with a cheerful goodbye. Either his old friend had an acting ability that he'd never revealed before, or he quite genuinely had no knowledge of what lay beneath the tarpaulin. Then again, was it not the case that people had a remarkable capacity for denial?

Iain left the house and began climbing the incline towards the cliffs. Wellingtons weren't the ideal footwear, but the rubber soles gripped into the peaty earth and he didn't slip, although his calves tugged tight. As he reached the first hill peak he paused to regain his breath. To his right, the west, he could see the offshore islands rising from the water like the humps of a monster. To his left, eastward, the green and grey of the island and houses like mere dots of white set against the magnitude of the land. How slight they were. How tenacious the people.

The struggle was different now. The drystane dykes of old, so skilfully built and maintained, falling into disrepair. Wild grass where once there had been oats and corn and potatoes. Dried-out peat banks. Cow sheds and barns falling in on themselves. Rusted brown scythes and ploughs lying abandoned in forgotten corners of the crofts. Wire fences hanging slack. Why endure the constant labour and expose yourself to the vagaries of the seasons when a steady job elsewhere could guarantee food, water and power? That had been the driving force behind the expansion of the towns and cities that had sucked so many of the rural young away. The islands had been slower to follow, but follow they inevitably had. The old ways were long gone and employment and pay were the priorities now. But as they had gone through famine before, so they were going through slump now. The mode of predicament might change, but always the islander faced the dilemma – whether to stay or go.

Cartographers considered the bay so insignificant that it barely merited an indent on the maps. Only the most detailed marked it, and yet what a history it had! Its union with mankind stretched across millennia. Those who lived here had survived only by respecting the forces around them.

As Iain walked along the cliff tops, the old stories sprang again to his mind. Here at the ravine of red rock a Norwegian schooner had run aground at the turn of the century.

'It was a ghost ship,' his grandfather would say. 'Not a soul on board. They thought it might be carrying the plague.'

His three grandchildren, Iain, Kenny and Christine, had listened, mouths open.

'Two men went out on a boat and all they could hear was the ring, ring of a bell. Oh, but they were brave men for going out. They climbed aboard and do you know what they saw?'

In his mind's eye, Iain saw the three listeners, all bursting in anticipation.

'I'll tell you that tomorrow night,' the old man had teased, his bushy white beard disguising the mirth in his face, but the twinkle in eyes giving him away.

'Oh, Grampa!' they had chorused in dismay.

He had prolonged the teasing for a few moments before pretending to succumb.

'Oh, very well. They found... Nothing! Not a soul.'

The children had gasped.

'And only later was it learned that the crew had abandoned the ship because they thought she was sinking. They landed safely and their boat sailed away on its own, right into the bay. But with no one to steer it, it crashed onto the rocks. Well, the crew, big blond men they were, they came in another boat to salvage what they could. What they couldn't take with them, the people of the village used. The ship was there for many's a year and do you know that some young boys used to use it for fishing. Do you know who one of these boys was?'

The children clung to his every word.

'It was me!' laughed the old man, seeing the amazement in their faces. 'I used to be a child just like you. Now your mother wants you in bed. Off you go.'

Iain smiled at the memory. The old man was a great one for his stories. Iain had grown sceptical of them, but as he got older he had learned that they were all based on truth.

At the places where it was possible to look over the cliffs, he did so. He wasn't sure what he expected to see and what he could do if the missing hiker had fallen.

By now he had reached the headland. Two centuries before, another ship had been smashed against the rocks in the next cove. The crew had got off but the captain had remained with his ship. It was his grave that was covered by the slab of rock on the moor. The rest of the crew had sought help in the village and it was said that some of them had settled there. Some might even be his own ancestors.

So much of the history around him was obscured by legend and rumour, with little hard fact to establish what had really happened. Would that be the destiny of the skeleton lying in the old house? That the truth of fate would never be known?

Chapter Twelve

IAIN HAD LOST himself on the moor, not literally, but meditatively. He glanced at his watch, surprised so much time had passed when all he'd done was sit on a rock watching the sea, listening to the wind and the birds.

Mary was sitting by the stove on his return, looking solemn.

'Why so serious?' he asked cheerfully, taking off his jacket.

'Iain a' ghraidh, I need to ask you something.' She sighed. 'I need you to take me to the hospital tomorrow. Will that be alright?'

'The hospital? What's wrong?' He sat down heavily at the window.

'Will it be okay for you to come?'

'Of course, no question, but what's wrong?'

'I've been getting a bit forgetful. I didn't think anything of it, just that I was getting on. But I found myself one day not knowing how to make a pot of tea and that's when I realised I should see the doctor. He made me an appointment to go to the hospital.'

'Why didn't you say?'

'I forgot.'

There were tears in her eyes. The tick of the clock seemed very loud.

Iain recalled Neilie's comment in the bar about his mother needing him now. He'd almost forgotten it amid all the other things Neilie had said. He sat for a moment in stunned silence, then, gathering himself, he moved across and put his arm around her.

'Mam, you should have told me. Who else knows? Have you told Christine? Kenny? Neilie?'

'No, not a soul. Neilie took me to the doctor's that's all.'

'Look, Mam,' he said encouragingly, 'when they find out exactly what it is, they can get the treatment started right away.'

His mother sat upright, breathed in deeply and blinked away her tears.

'No, a' ghraidh. The doctor thinks it might be some sort of dementia, and there is no cure for that. Whatever happens will be the Lord's choosing. Now, d'you want some tea?'

Iain held his head in his hands as he tried to absorb what she'd said. He felt her fingers ruffle his hair, like she did when he was a wee boy hugging her legs for comfort.

'I didn't want to say until I knew exactly myself, but that means going to the hospital. And Iain, no one else must know. Not yet. You must promise me that. Your sister, she's got a good heart, but there would be such a fuss and she has her own ones to look after.'

He looked up and saw the sympathy in her face. She was feeling sorry for him. What strength of spirit. Love and admiration coursed through him. Everything had to be as she wanted, he must find the strength for that. It would be hard, pretending that nothing was wrong. But she wanted no fuss, no talk. She was so private. That was her coping mechanism.

It had been the same when his father fell ill. Life had gone on as normal for as long as it could until he had become bedridden. And even then, even then, she showed only her familiar face to the world. It had been hard for those close to her. Iain remembered Christine, his sister, sobbing so sorely to him that she wanted to talk to her mother, to give voice to the fears and sorrow that were bound tight inside her.

Only when it was all over and his father had coughed his last did Mary speak, but only on her own terms. She would reminisce and sometimes express what her husband's opinion would have been on a given issue. She could speak of his death, but only after the fact. It was her way and for now it must be Iain's too.

The rain came in heavy that evening, blurring the windows. Iain agitated for the hours to pass, for night to fall and sleep to come, so that tomorrow would arrive sooner and the uncertainty would be gone. Not knowing infected every thought with dread and as soon as his mind found any distraction, the anxiety would resurface. Doubt played cruel games. At least knowledge provided a base from which real choices could be made.

When Christine had phoned, she could never have guessed what was going on. Her mother said the usual things. All was well, Iain was keeping himself busy, what about the children? How had school been today?

Iain realised it had been the same for him when he had come off the phone to her. Yes, there might be the occasional sore throat or cough that she would admit to, but now he asked himself how often there might have been other things that she had kept to herself. He would never know.

Since his return, he had become familiar with her evening routine. The television was a regular companion. *Coronation Street* was a favourite, a glimpse of life so different. When it was over, a cup of tea and her knitting and by the time the lamps of the house were on, she would turn to a magazine or a book. If her mind was troubled there was generally no sign of it. Throughout these evenings there would be snippets of conversation with Iain – an anecdote about Christine's children, the latest from the village, and oh, wasn't that character in the soap opera a bad man.

'Mam,' he reminded her, 'You said you had letters from Calum. Where are they?'

'Now,' she said, 'where did I put them? They must be in my wardrobe, in a blue and white box.'

It was strange going into his mother's bedroom. When he was a child, he was in and out of this room like any other in the house. After his marriage there had been the subtle change to being a visitor. It was a change of his own making and his parents had certainly never made him feel it, but this wasn't his home, not any longer. And with that perception came self-imposed restrictions. What reason could he have for going into their bedroom? When he was young he had liked watching the sunset from their room and he would sometimes lie across their bed reading a book. He couldn't do that now. It would have seemed inappropriate to himself. It's not that he never went in, but it was always for a specific reason.

Dark wooden wardrobes and the smell of perfume and talcum powder. Her dressing-table against the far wall, three shaped mirrors, one larger and two hinged to either flank spread across the full width, a cover of ivory lace on the highly polished wooden surface. Her jewellery box lay open. He could see her collection of brooches and a string of mother of pearl spilling out. Her wedding photograph in a sturdy wooden frame. Her bed with blankets and a heavy quilt, the pillows neatly stacked at the carved wood headboard. Beneath the window, the ottoman draped with a crochet cover of red lilies. Next to the bed on what had been his father's side, a high-backed chair with a cushioned leather seat. On his mother's side, a bedside cabinet covered by a lace cloth. A lamp with a large, conical shade. Her Bible. Blister packs of pills.

It was much as it had always been, but the old Westclox had been replaced by a white plastic radio alarm. It lacked the charm of the old one, but its large red numbers were bold and clear whatever the time of night. Framed photos hung on the wall above the headboard, showing grandchildren at various stages of development, all smartly dressed for the studio portraits. Once it had been photos of her own children that had hung there, but they were now displayed elsewhere in the house. It was these small differences that he noticed.

The wardrobes stood against the long outside wall at the foot of the bed. An old suitcase sat on top of each one which detracted from the aesthetic, but added to the character.

He couldn't open the door fully, but he could see a small pile of boxes beneath the dresses and coats. Mary had said a blue and white box. The only one matching that description was a highly decorative cardboard box, light blue with swirls of white.

He manoeuvred it out and carried it back through to the living room. The television was back on for the news, but Mary's head was down as she stitched and purled with her knitting needles.

'What used to be in this?' he asked, curious.

She looked up with interrupting her knitting.

'I got that on my Twenty-first. It was a brush and mirror

set. Oh but they were lovely. They're still there in one of the drawers.'

He put the box on the floor and lifted off the lid. It was so full that papers immediately slipped onto the carpet.

'These are all letters going back over the years. I've even got some from yourself when you were at the university. There are some from your father, some from Calum,' said his mother. 'I thought maybe if you look at them now and I can answer any questions while I'm able.'

The letters were stacked inside in no particular order. Iain picked up a couple of them. They were still in their envelopes, fading to yellow, with postmarks from forty years before. He picked up one, the purple stamp with the King's head postmarked 1936.

'I didn't know you had all these. I thought everything was in the box with the photos.'

'It's a long time since I looked at them.'

'Some of these are really old,' said Iain with wonder, glancing through another bundle. 'Look at this one. 1924!'

'That was my father. He was on the mainland trying to get a job then.'

'This one's got Dad's writing. What date's that? 1942.'

'He was in the Navy.'

'I never knew Dad to write a letter. Never.'

'Oh, he did,' smiled his mother. 'He could write a nice letter.'

'Can I look?'

'Yes,' she said. 'No secrets there.'

The letter had been written in pencil and the writing, although neat, didn't flow. His father was clearly unaccustomed to the practice and had laboured carefully over each word. The language was formal, but affectionate. It was a sailor missing his girl and telling her so. The simplicity and honesty of it brought tears to Iain's eyes.

'The old man, eh? I'd never have thought it.'

'We had lives before you boys and Christine came along, you know.'

'I know that. Of course. It's just that I never saw that side of him.'

'He was a loving father to you.'

'I know. But he wasn't a great one for showing affection.'

'Oh, he was affectionate, but things were different then. People showed it differently. But he loved his family and I never had cause to doubt that for one moment of the time we had together.'

'I know, Mam, I know.'

His eye caught another envelope with the number of the old house. It was addressed to his great-grandmother. Mary saw the eagerness in his face.

'That was from Calum to his mother,' she explained. 'He always took the time to write to her, although I think some of his letters must have been lost.'

The paper was no longer crisp, but the ink script, although pale, was legible.

Mary got up stiffly and went through to the kitchen. Iain started to read through the letter that Calum had sent all those years before.

He asked how she was keeping and how all the family were. What was the news from the village? He mentioned a couple of friends by name and wondered whether they had settled yet. The corn would be gathered soon, how had the crop been? And the cow, and the sheep? Was she managing to the church? How was she sleeping? He wanted to know everything that was happening in the place he still regarded as home. And he was concerned for his mother's welfare.

He asked how little Mary was doing. Was her hair still so blonde and when was she starting the school? Little Mary. The girl of whom he wrote could only be Iain's mother. Little Mary with the fair hair. 'She's such a pretty little thing in the photograph,' wrote Calum. As she had said to Iain just moments before, she had lived a life before her children were born. Sometimes that was easily forgotten.

Iain could picture her now, the bonny little girl playing around her grandmother's house, the apple of her granny's eye. She was the first of the grandchildren, and how she would have been adored by her uncles and aunts. What presents they would have brought from their travels to town or to the mainland! Somehow he imagined her in a white dress, though he knew that most of the children of the time wore home-made, hand-me-down clothes. Few even had shoes.

A lifetime on, it was all so different. She lived alone, her family was scattered, her own children away and her siblings either dead or a day's travel distant. It was the natural passage of life. She had often spoken to him of that. You loved what you had while you had it and then when it was gone, there was no reproach. She accepted change better than he did.

Calum wrote little of his own life: 'The job is going well.' His digs were 'swell'. He was eating heartily and had met some other Lewis boys, so his mother had nothing to be concerned about. He hoped, too, that the money he had sent would be helpful. He was her loving son and he would write again soon.

'Is that still Calum's letter you're reading?'

Mary had come back through with a tray of tea and biscuits. Iain carefully gathered the letters into a bundle and placed them on the floor, giving her room to sit down.

'He never saw his mother again after he left, did he?'

'No. Few of them ever saw their families again. They knew that when they left. That's why it was so hard. Some came home because it didn't work out for them, but most of them never came back. At least not until they were a lot older. Sometimes I wonder if they were ashamed to.'

'How d'you mean?'

'Well, a lot of them married boys and girls from the island who'd gone over there. But not all of them. There was a fellow from the village who worked in insurance and married well-to-do. He'd come from a poor household, most of them were, of course. My own mother used to say he could have have come back easily, but he never did. He sent money, but he never came home. Maybe he didn't want his wife to see where he came from. Well, there was no inside toilet for a start. How was a rich American girl going to cope with that?' She laughed gently at the image.

'Calum talks about "little Mary".'

'Yes, that was me. Little Mary. I was so fair then.'

'That's what he says.'

'It's getting lighter again,' she smiled touching her grey hair.

'It must have been a happy time.'

'Well maybe, but sadness was never far away. Calum, for a start. When he left, my granny knew she wouldn't see her own son again. Her own boy. When you think what that must have been like. I was tearful enough when you left for the university, but I knew you'd be back soon enough with that bag of yours filled with laundry.'

Mother and son chuckled.

'And there wasn't the same medical care,' she continued. People died of so many diseases that they can cure now.

The TB. So many died from that. You heard of someone with TB and you could see the heads shaking. And of course, there was the war. So they had happy times, but my, there were sad ones too.'

'It seems to have been much more of a community in those days.'

'Oh, there was always someone coming and going and people visiting. I miss that, right enough. I hardly see anyone these days. So many of the houses are empty. Between here and the shore there's what, five? six? All of them empty.'

'But you're not lonely, Mam, are you? You're never in!'

'I get out when I can, but the winters are long. It'd be wrong to think that everything was better back then, because it wasn't. It could be very hard. What I miss most is the people. There's far more that's gone than are left. That's what happens when you get to my age.'

'You can't live in the past though, Mam. You've always told me that yourself.'

'Nobody could accuse me of that. Isn't it yourself who's building the old house again? I think it's you who's thinking it was such a better time.'

'Building the house isn't living in the past. It's looking to the future, if anything.'

'Maybe you're right. Things change so fast. Nothing stays the same and you can't try to make it the same again. It never is.'

He recognised more of Calum's letters, selected them all from the box, five altogether, and sat back to read them properly.

One, sent from Toronto, Canada and dated May 1923, was the only letter in which Calum wrote in detail of his own experiences. He spoke of his sadness when the

Metagama sailed past Ness, the last sight of Lewis. Fires burned in farewell, lit by people watching the young blood of their island pour away once again. 'I must admit, Mother dear, that there were tears in my eyes and of most of my shipmates too.'

The crossing to Canada took more than a week. 'The sea wasn't so bad, but the icebergs were quite a sight to see!' They had landed in Newfoundland and had been taken to Toronto by train. From there the emigrants spread to all points west.

Another letter had been posted from a small town in Ontario. Calum was working on a farm. 'Not like the crofting,' he had noted. A third, dated two years later, had an address in Duluth in the United States. There wasn't any explanation of how he had come to be there. Perhaps that had been detailed in another letter, lost somewhere. His job, he told his mother, offered great opportunities, although he missed working in the open air.

'Mother dearest, I have taken up with a lovely girl and we have become very close,' was the disclosure in the fourth letter. 'I know you would like her. She is from a good, God-fearing family and she makes me very happy.'

The final letter in the series was from some years later. Calum wrote of how his children were growing and how one in particular carried the look of his mother's family. But he was more concerned with her well-being: 'You must take care of yourself, mother dear. Murdina and Mary tell me that you are not doing everything that the doctor tells you.'

Iain put the letters back in the box. It had been a fascinating glimpse of a life so different. Something troubled him, though, a niggling doubt that he couldn't isolate. It dwelt at the back of his mind like a shadow. Was there really something hidden in that dark corner of his consciousness or was it just his brain feeding on more doubt?

Later, as he lay in his bed and listened to his mother moving about downstairs, Iain thought of what she might have to endure and he sobbed for her. His cheeks were still damp when sleep claimed him.

Mary woke him with his usual breakfast. She'd put on a crisp, white blouse and the smart skirt of dark tartan that she wore to church. Her hair had been washed and set. She was ready to go.

'Oh Mam, I'm sorry,' he said glancing at the clock, thinking he'd slept in.

'No, no, there's plenty of time yet.'

There was too, at least two hours before they would need to go.

'What time did you get up?'

'I didn't really sleep much.' She looked out of his window. 'It's a lovely day. If you want to get work done at the house I'll get the bus over to town.'

'Don't be daft.'

'There was a helicopter out this morning, down by the shore. I wonder if they're looking for that camper?'

'Probably. That policeman said he was going to get onto the coastguard.'

'It didn't land, but I saw it passing up and down once or twice.'

'It's better that they didn't find anything.'

'Yes. I'm sure he'll be alright.'

They left earlier than necessary because, although she never said, Iain knew Mary would want to be at the hospital in plenty of time. The sun was up and the puffs of breeze were gentle. It was a day for living.

She sat next to him in the car with her good coat on, her handbag clasped on her lap and smelling faintly of her perfume. He didn't know what scent it was, probably a Christmas gift set from the grandchildren. Certainly it would have been too cheap for Yvonne, but it smelt so sweet on his mother.

'Are you set?'

'Yes, a' ghraidh.'

He clicked in a compilation tape of her favourite Gaelic soloists and drove down the hill on the single track road along which, generations apart, they'd both walked to school. The lochs were glinting. Moorland flowers danced in the wind, colourful bobs of yellow and purple, and sheep calmly munched the grass, unperturbed. Birds flitted back and forth above the grasses, their chirping lost beneath the hum of the engine and the songs of lost love.

The journey over to town normally took Iain little more than half an hour, less if he really hit the floor, but he knew that would make his mother even tenser and they had plenty of time.

It was almost a mile to the bridge across the river and the junction that would take them onto the double track road to town. They passed through villages with Norse names and empty houses and saw old Maggie Magnus walking stiffly down the track to her gate. She flapped her hand in recognition as they drove by.

They could see the ancient stones of Calanais standing on the skyline, brooding and mysterious. This was as far inland as the sea stretched, and the mass of the moor rolled away north and south to the hills of Uig and Harris. Lochs studded the green like dark diamonds.

The road cut across the midriff of the island through Lochganvich and Achmore, the only villages not tied to the sea. They had originally been settled by destitute people cleared from coastal townships. At the junction with the road that stretched south to the very tip of Harris, Iain took a left, north to Stornoway.

Soon it was possible to glimpse the war memorial, a stone tower built to commemorate those who never came home. Beyond shimmered the Minch and the mountains of Wester Ross shaded the horizon a faint purple.

The approach to town was like nowhere else on the island, with the wooded castle grounds that had given generations of islanders their first sight of trees. It was said that one Harrisman had marvelled at the size of the potato plants here. Iain doubted the truth of it, but it was always a tale to tell.

The tape finished. He moved his hand to change it over, but Mary said, 'Leave it. I'll enjoy the rest going back home.'

The hospital was on the outskirts of town. As they drove into the car park, She turned to him.

'I don't want you waiting with me. It's just a chat with the specialist. You go into town and do any business you need to do.'

'Don't be silly, Mam.'

'I mean it, Iain.' The use of his name underlined her insistence. 'I don't want to think you are sitting around worrying.'

'There's nothing to worry about.'

'You might be right, but that's what we'll find out. I would prefer you came back for me rather than sitting around.'

She could see him looking at her uncertainly.

'Please, Iain. It would make me feel better.'

With a shake of his head, Iain jumped out of the car to open her door for her. As she pulled herself out, she smiled. 'I haven't reached that stage yet.' She carried her old leather handbag and wore her best shoes, with their small square heels. He noticed a crease was forming against the strain of the bunion on her right foot.

He stood beside her as she checked in at the reception and accompanied her along to the waiting bay. Eventually a nurse called her name and smiled encouragingly at her.

She turned to him, 'Now, I told you to go.' Her tone was firm.

He watched her disappear down the brightly lit corridor on the arm of the nurse, her dignity intact.

Stornoway was its usual bustle, with the cars and vans cruising up and down Cromwell Street. Iain parked in the car park on South Beach. The air was strong with the smell of fish from the trawlers berthed at the quay. Seagulls flocked everywhere. There were harassed mothers with young children in prams, workmen in boiler suits and steel-capped boots, elderly folk chatting, some tourists. But for the changing styles of clothes and cars it could have been twenty, even forty years ago. It had been the same the day before Rob was lost, and the day after. It would be like this today and tomorrow, irrespective of what news his mother received. The traumas of small lives played out against a backdrop in which only the fine details changed.

He wandered in towards the town's heart, The Narrows, a familiar haunt from his schooldays. There was not a face he recognised.

'Mr Martin?' said a voice beside him.

It was the archaeologist, emerging from a shop.

'Melanie. Melanie Russell.' She beamed at him.

'Yes, I know who you are,' he said politely. There could be only one reason she was speaking to him. 'Have you had any news about the bone?'

'No, nothing definite yet, but I'm intrigued.'

'Believe me,' laughed Iain, hiding his nervousness, 'so am I. I was going for a coffee. Would you like one?'

He didn't know where the impulse had come from. Perhaps it was the warmth in her dark eyes. Curiosity, attraction, the need for company? Whatever the reason, he felt a blush burning his face.

'Yes, that would be lovely.'

The tightness was in his throat again and he didn't know what to say next.

'There's a place back there,' she said. He liked the smile in her voice. 'Is that where you were going?'

'Why not?'

'I'll just put my shopping in the car,' she said.

'Here, let me help.' A voice from his past came to life in his head, critical of his every utterance, cursing him as a fool and making him self-conscious of every movement.

They carried the bags to her car and then made their way to the coffee shop, agreeing on what a lovely day it was. They sat opposite each other at a small table and a waitress brought their order.

'I don't understand how that bone came to be on its own,' Melanie said just before placing her lips against a steaming mug of milky coffee.

'You and me both.'

'Even when we dig in ancient sites and come across something like that, there is usually something else to be found.'

Not for the first time, Iain wondered why he still had

felt driven to lie about the skeleton. And if he wanted it to remain secret, why had he handed over the bone to this woman? He didn't make sense to himself. What was it Yvonne had called him? Conflicted? He pulled his mind back to Melanie's interrogation.

'There was definitely nothing else?'

'I didn't dig around much, but nothing that I could see.'

'I would guess it's up to fifty years old. That's not old. We're not talking about battle sites, and I assume it's not a graveyard, so how did it get there?'

Iain shrugged his shoulders.

'Would you mind if I came to see the site sometime? What exactly is it anyway?'

'It's an old house I'm renovating.'

'Oh really! How exciting!'

'I'm not so sure.'

'Why not?'

'I haven't a clue what I'm doing for a start. And anyone who does tells me I'm daft.'

'Oh no. It sounds a marvellous idea.'

'That's the thing. The idea might sound great, but not the putting it into action. I'm beginning to have my own doubts.'

'Is it just that you wanted a place to stay?'

'It's more than that. It's about reconnecting with my roots, bringing the place back to life. Crazy when you think about it.'

'Not at all. It takes thinking like that to make places special. If we all built timber-frame and breeze block, what would we have?'

'Comfortable houses,' he smiled. 'Maybe I'm not going to abandon it, but I need to plan properly. I've gone into this blind, thinking that determination would do. It won't.'

'You're living in another place now though?'

'Yes, with my mother.'

She smiled knowingly, her hair falling over her face a little as she tried to hide it.

'I've been in Glasgow for a few years,' he explained defensively. 'I've just come home.'

'Why?'

'Since you ask,' he confided, not fully understanding why, 'my marriage collapsed and my job disappeared.'

'I'm sorry. I didn't mean to pry.'

'It's no big secret.'

'That must have been awful.'

'I've had better years.'

Her head was tilted at an angle now, her eyes narrowed appraisingly.

'I suppose,' he explained, 'I suppose it was always going to happen. Neither was right for me.' His fingers fiddled with a sugar sachet.

'And what is right for you?'

'That's what I'm finding out.' He met her eyes. 'Being here for a start, being on the island.'

After a moment she asked, 'And the house is part of that?'

'I had hoped so. Maybe not.'

There was a silence. Iain felt disturbed and excited. Was he kidding himself? Everything about her indicated warmth returned, her smile and the shyness about meeting his eyes for too long. She broke the spell.

'Is the house where you found the bone?'

'Yes.'

'How could a human bone end up in a house? That sounds so suspicious.'

'I've never said it wasn't.'

'Have you got the police involved yet?'

'No. I haven't been sure what to do. And if you're saying the bone could be fifty years old there's not much the police could do about it now. I was waiting until I heard from you before deciding what to do.'

Melanie looked at her watch, a big dial on a small strap.

'I have to get going, but I would really like to see what you discovered. Would it be okay if I came out to see it sometime?'

'Of course.'

'Thank you for the coffee,' she smiled as she got up to go.

'I'll call you to arrange a visit?'

She left the café, looking over her shoulder with a smile and a shy wave.

He pushed his hand back through his hair and sighed. This had crept up on him and he didn't know how to deal with it. It was nearly twenty years since he had been involved in the dating game and he didn't know where to start any more. His heart sank as he realised that she had said she'd call him, but hadn't asked for his number. Then he remembered she'd taken a note of it when he first saw her in Uig. There it was already, the roller-coaster of emotion.

There was still some time before he was expected back at the hospital. He took the opportunity to go into the library and approached the desk with a request for newspapers from the time of Rob's death. The librarian disappeared into a storeroom, eventually returning with a large, leather-bound volume of the *Gazette*, with the paper's title and year embossed on the front.

He soon found the edition he was looking for. The date

was one he would never forget. There it was, a few short paragraphs at the foot of the centre column. The small headline told all there was to tell, 'Island Boy Missing at Sea'. The story had broken close to the paper's print deadline and there was no picture of Rob.

Hopes are fading for an island youth who has been missing since Tuesday's storm. 19-year-old Robert Morrison from Carloway had been fishing in East Loch Roag. He was swept overboard from his rowing boat while heading back to shore. Searches by the coastguard and local boats have failed to find any trace of him. His companion, 19-year-old Neil Smith, was rescued and treated for shock. A spokesman for the coastguard said, 'We will keep looking, but as time passes we must prepare for the worst.'

Less than a hundred words. A couple of phone calls and the paragraphs would have been typed up in time for the deadline. The reporter had done his job. What the story didn't tell, was the anguish behind the stark facts; a family's crushing grief, the life now nothing more than memories in a mother's heart, the elusive images in the recollections of friends, the future that would now never be.

Iain didn't know what he had expected to find. A detail, perhaps, that had been forgotten over the years, but which might have clarified the mystery. There was none. He flicked through subsequent issues, but there was no further mention of Rob. No body had been found and by the following week and the ending of the official search it was old news.

He knew that if he had taken out the issues for the following year he would have found in the 'In Memoriam' section of the paper, one intimation from Rob's parents remembering their loving son, safe now with the Lord and another from Rob's friends that he and Neilie had composed. He recalled how they had spent an evening with a notepad and pen, scribbling, scoring out and rewriting. They had set out with the intention of getting away from the conventional sentimental passages to convey the real meaning of his friendship. Song lyrics were the most obvious source of inspiration, and they tried out so many, from the Beatles, the Stones, Simon and Garfunkel. Neilie had been keen on a line from *Yesterday*, but it didn't match precisely and to have adapted it would have looked trite. The discussion had knocked back and forth and in the end they could agree on nothing. Iain couldn't recall the exact words they used in their message, but its distinction was its brevity, a sentence of tribute and their names.

He would have checked it out, but he had to get back to the hospital. On no account could he be late. As he drove through town he couldn't get Melanie out of his mind and he felt guilty about it. His focus should be entirely on his mother.

The teenagers from the high school were gathered around The Narrows during the lunch hour, flirting, posing, bragging, bantering. They were all young enough to be his children and yet their preoccupations were the same as his. He fancied Melanie. It was as simple and embarrassing as that. He had no idea what to do about it. And he could not forget Catriona, however much he might try to. Alone in the car, he felt himself blush with confusion.

He saw his mother coming towards him as soon as he arrived. She was with the same nurse he'd seen before and was speaking quite easily to her. There was no clue from

her manner as to how she had got on. Perhaps she was
gripping her handbag more tightly.

She gave Iain a close-mouthed smile, before turning back
to the nurse.

'Thank you, dear.'

'Have you been waiting long?' he asked anxiously.

'No, no. That's me just finished now.'

'How did you get on?' He tried not to sound impatient.

'Well, a' ghraidh, we'll need to see.'

'What?' The frustration burst through.

'They asked me a lot of questions and the consultant
wants you to come with me the next time, if you can
manage. Oh but he was a nice man. He said that from
what the doctor said and what he saw himself, that they've
probably got it early.'

'Oh well that's good news,' Iain exhaled, unaware he'd
been holding his breath.

'Yes, but he said he didn't want to make any promises.
He said I shouldn't worry myself too much, sometimes it
takes a long time before it gets bad.'

'You'll get all the care you need, Mam, you know that.'

'I told him my son was with me and he seemed to be
happy about that.'

They reached the car and Mary didn't quibble when he
opened the door and helped her in. Soon they were on the
road. He assailed her with questions about what else the
consultant had said. As they drove past Marybank and
away from the town he could tell she was weary. He clicked
on the cassette and an unaccompanied voice sang an
émigré's song. His mother sat again with her handbag
clasped on her lap, her eyes looking westward and home.

Chapter Thirteen

MARY HAD SAT through the whole journey listening to the songs on the cassette, some of which she would have first heard at her mother's knee.

When they got home she had gone for a nap, but she was up later in the afternoon and insisted on making dinner. Nothing would be gained from sitting around. 'That would be the first sign of defeat,' she told him.

Yvonne rang as he sat reading his paper.

'Iain?'

He was surprised to hear her voice.

'Yes.' He paused and continued without conviction. 'It's good to hear from you.'

'Are you coming down?' she continued. 'We've got a firm offer for the house, despite your junk lying around, but it's conditional on them getting in quickly. I want to get it all cleared up before I go to London, so we have to move fast. There are some papers you need to sign. I could post them, but by the time you got them and sent them back it'd be cutting things a bit fine. And you'll have to clear out your stuff. I don't know what you want done with it.'

'Uh-uh,' said Iain cautiously.

'You've forgotten, haven't you? I knew you would.' She was very irritated.

'No, no, I'm booked to fly out tomorrow,' he said defensively, hoping the flight wasn't full.

'Oh. I'm sorry, but you didn't let me know. I thought

you were being your usual.'

There had been little animosity in the practical, final stages of the breakdown of their marriage. The resentment had mostly been consumed in the constant carping that gradually eroded their feelings for each other. Prime among his faults was a lack of verve, which Yvonne had once considered to be a laid-back cool. Now, she assumed, correctly, that he had forgotten to do something he'd promised. His usual tactic in these circumstances was to bluff it out.

'I'll be there tomorrow.'

'Good.' Yvonne's tone softened.

'Where will I meet you? The lawyer's?'

'No, At the house. The flight should get you in before lunchtime.'

There was nothing to beat travelling to and from the islands by road and sea: the hypnotic effect of watching the wash created by the ferry cutting through the Minch; the changing landscapes through the rugged, ragged, western Highlands, the rolling greenery of Perthshire and finally the urban central belt. But it took the best part of a day. The flight took less than an hour.

There was plenty of room on board the twin turboprop aircraft. Given the inflated prices charged, that was no surprise. It was cheaper to fly the Atlantic. The other passengers were mostly men in suits, businessmen, officials of one sort or another and a couple of ministers. There was a ruddy, tweedy man with a signet ring, a paid up member of the huntin', fishin', shootin' brigade, Iain observed. Another distinct group were the offshore workers, men with the look of the outdoors about them. An elderly man, clearly bound for a funeral, kept his black hat on throughout the flight. There were one or two older women, not unlike his own mother, going to visit their families.

Iain's seat was just in front of the wing. The propeller vanes that obstructed his view disappeared when the engines kicked into life. The plane droned towards the end of the runway, then in a rush of power, soared skyward.

The landscape shimmered with the lochs and pools diffused across it. It was as if the sea was springing up through leaks in the earth. From the air, you could see the interior of the island and how much remained unseen from the spindly roads that spread out from town. Within moments they were over water, the green land and the purple rock falling away behind, seemingly slipping into the dark sea. Ten minutes later, the seaway that took more than three hours to ply by ferry had been crossed and the mountains of Wester Ross, a maze of gorges, glens and fissures lay beneath them.

How empty Scotland was. Little communities lost in pleats of land, or on the fringes of the ocean. And away from the coasts and the rivers nothing but forest, moor, and the chasms carved by the great bergs of the ice age.

Kings and Queens had murdered for this land, nobles had betrayed their own, the people had repelled and been overwhelmed by invaders. Yet could now be spanned in no time.

The plane landed at Glasgow on schedule. Iain had no luggage and so he went straight through the airport for a taxi. The motorway was free-flowing and within twenty minutes he was standing outside his house. The gate needed oiling, the grass on the front lawn needed mowing and the flower beds were already being colonised by weeds. He turned the brass knob of the front door. It was unlocked.

Yvonne must be here already.

'Hello!' he called.

She came walking through from the kitchen. She was dressed rather formally, in a long-sleeved blouse and well cut trousers. The 'G' in the buckle of the belt should mean something, he knew that, but he didn't know what.

'Hi,' she said, turning into the front lounge. He followed.

It was the familiar room, carpet and wallpaper, but except for the suite and the coffee table everything else was gone. The television, the paintings on the wall, the ornaments and books.

Sheets of paper were spread over the coffee table. Yvonne sat down on the edge of one armchair. The jacket that matched the trousers was folded over the back of the chair.

'These are the papers I need you to sign,' she indicated, taking a pen from her briefcase. She knew there was little chance of him having one.

Iain scribbled his name at the places marked x. Yvonne gathered the papers up and checked them over. Iain watched her closely. Her hair had been restyled away from the soft fringe she'd had for the past few years to a fuller, longer, style. It was a classier, more mature look and it suited her. Her make-up was carefully applied, the shades more subtle than before. Yvonne had always aspired to an image with which he had never been comfortable; at one time she had even gone to the extent of choosing his clothes for him. Freed from his limiting factor, she was emerging as the woman she wanted to be.

'Well that seems to be it,' she said brusquely. 'That wasn't so hard, was it?'

'You're looking well,' he said.

'Thank you. Now, I don't know what you'll think of this idea, but I've got a hire car, it's a big estate. What would you say to loading your boxes into it and then we could take them to a storage depot. You can leave everything until you decide what you're going to do.'

He shrugged, ostentatiously casual.

'I'll get this back to the lawyers and come back for you. What do you say?'

'Yes, fine.'

She stood up and slipped on her jacket.

'They're in the spare room, okay?' She left before he could even get out of the seat.

There were six thick cardboard boxes, approximately three feet by two by one and a half. Yvonne had brought them to the house. In fact there was very little he had done as their marriage wound to its close. He'd filled some of them himself before heading north, expecting to have plenty of time to come back and finish the job, but she had completed it for him. Three contained his albums and another two were full of books and miscellaneous junk, papers and documents, including the graduation scroll of which his parents had been so proud. The final box held his treasured collection of music magazines. Lying open beside them were two suitcases containing all the clothes he'd left behind.

It wasn't much to show for the life he and Yvonne had shared together. When the final break came he had lived there alone while She went to her parents. It was agreed that she dispose of what she could. Three times he had been surprised by strangers calling to remove furniture. The dining-room table and chairs that Yvonne had been so eager to acquire was taken by a second-hand dealer and on another occasion Iain endured the indignity of a charity truck calling for the bedroom furniture. Maybe she had told him when they were coming, he couldn't remember. It wasn't worth the friction of querying it.

He carried the boxes downstairs to the empty hall and then sat and waited. One of the photos showed them as a happy couple just after their engagement. Yvonne was cuddling in to him. She was such a pretty girl. It dismayed him to think that he'd betrayed that innocence. Some of the time he couldn't face it. It was easier to blame her. But at this moment he couldn't avoid the fact that she had loved him very much. And he had been deeply fond of her. But that wasn't the same, it wasn't enough. The other side of it was that she had known his faults, even then, but had been determined to change him, to mould him into the husband she wanted him to be. The cracks had been there from the beginning. Maybe he wasn't entirely to blame, but it didn't make looking at that photograph any easier.

Yvonne was very pleased when she returned.

'Good, you're ready.'

He loaded the boxes into the car and she carried the suitcases. Mrs Syme would be watching it all through her net curtains. More to tell her friends.

'I think that's pretty well everything,' Yvonne said as she closed the boot. There was relief in her voice. Perhaps this was less of an ordeal than she had expected.

It was no great wrench to leave the house. The thrill of having secured this as their home had long since gone. Iain felt nothing for the place now.

As they drove down towards the river, he directed her to a warehouse where he knew there was a shipping agent.

'I'm as well to ship everything home. I'll probably stay there for a while until I think things through.'

'You're not planning to live there in the long term, are you?'

'I don't know. The thing is, my mother, well she's taken ill and I want to be with her for a while.'

'Oh. I'm sorry to hear that. Nothing serious, I hope.'

'It's dementia. Alzheimer's they think. It's still at an early stage. She's not too bad.'

'Your mother is strong, Iain,' Yvonne said, moving her hand from the gear stick to brush his arm. 'It can take years for it to get bad.'

Processing the boxes at the shipping agent took a while and it was well after lunch time by the time they were finished. They walked back towards the car.

'Have you got time for a bite to eat?' he asked her.

She was hesitant.

'I've got some things to do, but I could do with something to eat.'

He suggested a small bistro in the West End. Yvonne ordered pasta, he chose pizza. She told him quite matter-of-factly of all the arrangements she'd made, how he would get his share of the profits from the house and the furniture they'd sold. He trusted her to play it by the book, it was her way. After they'd eaten, he asked her about London. The job was a transfer within her own company and she had a flat organised for three months. She was looking forward to the challenge, but admitted to some nerves. Iain reassured her that she would do well, it was what she'd always wanted.

'I didn't try to hold you back, Yvonne. I just didn't try to do much of anything, I suppose,' he confessed.

'We've been through all that. We wanted different things and it's taken us a while to realise it. Better now than never.'

'I just don't want you thinking our life together was a waste. I don't want you leaving today thinking that.'

'I don't. We had a lot of happy times and we learned a lot together. Of course there's stuff I resent, but...' she couldn't complete the sentence.

Iain touched her hand.

'Let's look to the future. Here's to it.' They lifted their wine glasses and clinked them together. Yvonne was trying to smile, but tears were welling in her eyes. The practical persona was falling apart in front of him. He was struggling to control his own emotions.

'D'you want to hear about my troubles?' he asked in as light a tone as he could manage. Yvonne was pulling a paper hankie from her back and looked at him uncertainly.

'I've found a body. I have, honestly. And I haven't a clue what to do.' He was half-smiling at her now, feeling more in control.

'What are you talking about?' She looked incredulous.

'I'm telling you, Yvonne, I've found a body, a skeleton, and I don't know what to do about it.'

'A skeleton?'

'Honestly. You know the old house, down by the shore? Well I was digging there and I've uncovered a skeleton.'

'Whose is it? Do you know?'

'I don't. I've got some crazy ideas, but I don't actually know.'

'What have the police said?'

'They don't know.'

'You haven't told the police?'

'No.'

Yvonne's old lecturing tone was returning.

'Why not? Surely that's the first thing you should have done?'

'I'm not rightly sure. At first I thought it must be very old. I'm not so sure now, and it's become... a dilemma.'

'How?'

'This is going to sound daft, but you remember Rob?'

'Of course. You spoke about him a lot.'

'I'm really scared it's him.'

'How could it be? You said he drowned.'

'That's what I always thought, but I'm not so sure now and that's what's really worrying me. I always thought Neilie was in the boat with him, but it turns out he wasn't.'

'Nothing about Neilie would surprise me.' Yvonne had never hidden her contempt for Neilie. She'd always viewed him as another piece of grit irritating her marriage. Iain always got more drunk with him than anyone else.

'The point is that I haven't told anybody, but I'm sure Neilie has guessed what I've found. After all these years, he suddenly tells me he was never in the boat with Rob. Says they'd had a big row. Now I'm thinking that maybe he hasn't told me the whole story. Maybe the row became a fight and something nasty happened and Neilie tried to cover it up.'

'You don't think Neilie might have killed him?'

'Not deliberately, but he... Oh I don't know what to think. It doesn't make sense.'

'You know what I think of Neilie. He's always been trouble, and his wife didn't seem to care.'

'What's Cat got to do with it?' Iain instantly regretted defending her. Yvonne must have noticed.

'He's daft, but even I don't think he could do anything like that,' she said.

Iain rubbed his face and arched his back against his seat.

'But if that's what happened, and I tell the police, then

where does that leave everything?'

'Iain, listen, if he's done something he's got to pay for it. He can't just walk away from it. Who knows that he wouldn't do it again? You don't know that he hasn't. What are you protecting him for? Rob was your friend as well. Surely he deserves some justice?'

Iain was sitting forward again, rubbing his fingers across his forehead.

'Are you sure it's Rob? Have you found out for sure? Who else could it be?' Yvonne asked.

'That's the thing. There was this German guy, a camper, he was hanging around talking about his dead girlfriend, saying they came there all the time. The day after he realised I was digging about the house he disappeared. He's left everything behind, but there's no word on where he's gone.'

'Iain, you've let this go on too long. You should have gone to the police straight away. They'd be able to find out for sure how old the skeleton is and that might rule Rob out. Stop messing about trying to protect Neilie. If he did it then he deserves what's coming to him and if he didn't then you've got nothing to worry about.'

Iain finished his glass of wine, nodding. Everything she said made sense, of course it did.

'You'll need to get back for your flight,' said Yvonne. 'I'll give you a lift.'

They paid the bill and walked back to the car, through the area where they had done much of their dating. They didn't hold hands this time.

As Yvonne pulled into the traffic she suddenly asked, 'Why were you digging at the house in the first place?'

'What?'

'The house, why were you digging there?'

'I don't know, really. Curiosity I suppose.'

'You've not still got that mad idea of living there, have you?' she laughed.

'When did I say that?'

'You've mentioned it before when you've been getting carried away with yourself. You are, aren't you? You're thinking of staying there.'

'Okay, okay. The idea had crossed my mind.'

'Poor Iain,' she said, shaking her head. 'Always thinking that things were better before.'

As they approached the airport from the motorway Yvonne told him that she would drop him off at the apron, rather than parking.

'You'll be going straight in, anyway, and I've got some stuff to see to.'

It struck Iain that this could be the last time they saw each other for he didn't know how long. They had been moving steadily towards this moment for a couple of years now, but its imminence disturbed him. That and the fact that it would be necessarily cursory. His heart thudded as they pulled up.

'You look after yourself, Yvonne. I'll be thinking of you.'

'Will you?'

'Don't doubt it.'

'And you, get this thing sorted.'

He clicked off his seat belt and leaned over to kiss her cheek. It was flushed and warm.

'Take care of yourself. Keep in touch.'

She couldn't answer. He got out of the car without another word and watched as she pulled away. The last he saw was the back of her hand wiping across her eyes.

He felt morose sitting on the plane waiting to take off. Finally he had left his old life behind. There was no going back.

Iain sat deep in thought as the plane ploughed north by north-west, the landscape below now obscured by the mounds of cloud drifting from the south-west. In two days, Yvonne would be making her own flight in the opposite direction, south, to the concrete metropolis. He would be back on the sea-scarred island.

As the plane descended he could see far below a trawler bound for home, so flimsy and yet defiant. His own thoughts clarified too. Yvonne had been right. He must confront his fears and face them down.

Chapter Fourteen

DRIVING ACROSS THE island, Iain's spirits lifted. Yvonne had always said the island was fine, but what about theatre and restaurants and the other pleasures of city living? He understood the point of view, but here, every day, nature staged its own spectacular performance. And what could be better than the fresh seafood all around them? It was all a matter of perspective.

Mary was bright and told him she'd had a good day. She'd heard that the German lad was still missing. How was Yvonne and what was she doing with herself? Had everything gone according to plan?

Iain insisted that she phone Kenny and Christine and tell them the outcome of her hospital visit. They both asked to speak to him after she'd broken the news and their reactions were as he expected, Kenny quiet and tense, Christine insisting that she come home. It took him a while to convince her that that would not be necessary. At least it was out in the open. It was a time for establishing truths.

By early evening the clouds were a shade darker, but the sea remained calm. From his window Iain could see Neilie's van driving up the road home. It wouldn't be long before he would be knocking at the door. He'd always enjoyed his fishing had Neilie, and he had probably spent all day looking forward to going out in his boat.

The van reappeared half an hour later and drove past the house as if heading for the shore. It was another half hour before Neilie knocked on the door and strode into the house as jovial as ever.

'What's doing with you, Mary?'

'It's yourself, Neilie. Oh, nothing much. You're out on the water tonight?'

'Got to get your boy to catch a fish somehow. You'll have some cod for your dinner tomorrow, believe me.'

'That'll be lovely, but mind you take care.'

Iain appeared at the kitchen door, already prepared to go.

'You're set then?' said Neilie.

'Right, Mam, we'll be back by dark,' said Iain.

'With a bucketful of fish,' Neilie promised.

'Be careful.'

She waved to them from the door as they clumped along the road.

'Did I see you here earlier?' Iain asked.

'I was taking down all the gear. Saves us carrying it.'

'The forecast doesn't look so good.'

'Depends which one you listen to. There's a front moving in, but it won't be here until the morning.'

'Where are you thinking of going?'

'Not far out. Is there anywhere you want to go especially? What about round into the east loch?'

Iain shrugged and they walked a few more yards. The village was quiet. Braggan's loom was silent and there was no sound of children.

'What is it you wanted to ask me about the house?' asked Neilie.

'I'll show you when we get there.'

'It won't take too long, will it? We want to get out there.'

'It shouldn't.'

'I can tell you now, if you want to do it properly, you're going to have to flatten it and build it up again from scratch.

Think of it, you've only got one window in the place. You can make it bigger.'

Neilie kept offering help and advice.

'Like I said, I'll get a digger and I'll get it all flattened and prepared. Start fresh. You won't need the double wall. We'll build an inner wall of timber and line it all properly. It's only fit for sheep the way it is.'

They were near the house now. The tent was still there.

'That camper is still missing.' Neilie said. 'Doesn't look so good does it?'

They reached the doorway. Iain entered first and went straight over to the tarpaulin. He turned round, but Neilie hadn't followed.

'Neilie!'

There was no reply.

'Neilie!'

Still nothing.

He stepped quickly back to the door. Neilie was standing looking to sea. He turned as Iain approached.

'If we don't go now, cove, we're as well to forget it. That front's coming in quicker than I thought. C'mon, let's go.'

He made off down the brae to the boat.

Iain hesitated.

'Hurry up. We'll call in on the way back if you want. Let's get some fishing done.'

'No. You must see this.'

Neilie stopped in his tracks, turned and stomped belligerently back without saying a word. Iain kicked off some of the stones weighing down the tarpaulin and then, grasping a corner, he whipped it back, sending the other stones clattering against the walls.

'Look at that.'

Neilie walked slowly towards him, not able to see the skeleton at first. When he did he recoiled and groaned.

Iain pulled more of the canvas cover away.

'Is that what I'm thinking it is?'

'Yes. The question is, who is it?'

Neilie looked closely at Iain.

'Do you know?'

'Do you?'

'How the hell would I know?'

'I just thought you might have an idea.'

'I don't,' said Neilie, his eyes never leaving the remains before him. 'When did you find this?'

'A few days ago.'

'What have the police said?'

'I haven't told them yet.'

'You haven't told them?' Neilie caught Iain's eye for the first time.

'I haven't told anyone until now.'

'Why not?'

'I don't know. I wanted to talk to you first. See what you thought.'

Neilie looked again at the bones, almost motionless, his hands thrust deep into the pockets of his jacket. Then he sighed.

'There's only one thing you can do.'

Iain looked at him questioningly.

'You'll have to tell the police. Now, let's go fishing.'

With that he turned and walked out of the house. Iain stood where he was. It wasn't the reaction he had anticipated, but then he wasn't sure what he had expected. A whirl of scenarios had played before him, an emotional confession perhaps, or a violent denial, but there had been nothing, no emotion beyond the initial surprise. He didn't know what to make of it. The scene ran through his head again and then he laughed. Neilie couldn't know anything about it. Why should he? The whole thing had been exaggerated in his own mind? The emotional upheaval of the past days had stopped him thinking straight. There could be any number of explanations for a body being buried in a deserted house. It was sinister, yes, but he had been wrong just to look at his own close circle. Neilie was right, let the authorities deal with it.

By the time he had replaced the stones on the tarpaulin, Neilie was already onto the shingle.

'C'mon,' he shouted.

The sea was more agitated than it had been before, the water fizzing back through the pebbles. Neilie was pulling the boat towards him, its easy inertia providing token resistance, the water dripping off the rope as it dipped below the surface between pulls. Neilie's hands were roughened by physical graft, the nails broken and dirty, scars and scabs marking the countless cuts over the years. The dragging of the rope would have felt rough to Iain's softer skin, but Neilie was oblivious to the coarse fibres rasping over his calloused palms.

The keel of the boat scraped against the stones where they shelved up from the sea floor to the beach. Neilie waded out up to his thighs and grasped the bow. 'In you get,' he instructed.

Iain waded out and swung his leg over the side, the boat swaying feistily as he did so. It took him a couple of moments of comic clambering before he was fully aboard. He flopped flat, water running off his boots.

'That'll be you in then,' teased Neilie, pulling the bow round towards him and heaving himself into it in one easy motion.

'It's been a long time, cove, hasn't it? Looked like you were trying to mount a horse there. What are you looking for now?'

'A life-jacket.'

'A life-jacket?' scoffed Neilie. 'When have I ever carried one of them?'

'I know we didn't years ago, but I thought you would now.'

'Nah. I never go out very far.'

'That sky doesn't look promising.'

'We'll take the risk.'

Neilie tugged on the starter. It took a couple of yanks before the outboard motor kicked into life in a plume of exhaust fumes. He manoeuvred so that the bow was pointing away from the shore and then twisted the accelerator a little more. The boat rode up and down on the slight swell as it headed out to open sea.

Iain looked into the water and could see almost nothing through the deep, deep green but the occasional tress of seaweed. Waves smacked against the hull. They were already passing the teeth of rocks that protected the mouth of the bay. The movement of the sea became more pronounced.

The cliffs looked intimidating, a dramatic plunge as rock surrendered to ocean, the rends, ruptures and rubble evidence of the eternal and ferocious elemental conflict.

As they emerged from the bay into the Atlantic, Neilie turned left and south.

'Where are we headed?'

'Round the headland, like I told you. Out by the lighthouse, where we used to go. I was out there a few nights ago and there were so many biting I was having to throw them back. What's the matter? You look as if you're not enjoying it.'

'It's been a long time. I'm just getting used to it again.'

'Away with you, you're getting soft with all that city living. Make sure if you're sick you put it over the side. How often did we come out here before you left? You, me, Rob, Kenny, my old man and yours. Your old man loved it. And he was good too. Always seemed to know where to go and what to do. D'you remember that night he pulled in that basking shark? What a night that was! Bloody thing was snapping away like mad and we're stabbing everything at it. Blood was everywhere. And your old man is shouting at Kenny to bale out the blood. We had to throw it over the side, it was so big. What a waste. Some night, that! My mam thought I'd killed someone when I got back. If my dad hadn't been with us I don't think she'd have believed it.'

They both laughed at the memory.

'I'm not denying it, I was scared,' admitted Iain. 'It pierced my boot with its teeth, clean through. I'm lucky it never took the foot off me. All I got was a scrape on the ankle, but I had nightmares about that. A shark, for Christ's sake!'

'But the thing is, your old man was determined to bring it in. Me? I'd have cut the line, but no, he's hauling away at it and then my old man is by his side. Oh it was funny!'

'It is now, but I never went out much after that.'

'Surely that didn't put you off?'

'Not just that, but I've never been keen on the sea.'

'How can you not like the sea? You're a Leodhsadh. We're sailors. That's all we've ever been, sailors and fishermen. Who in your own family never went to sea?'

'I just don't like it. I can't understand why it doesn't scare you, after what happened.'

Neilie thought for a moment.

'It's what you know. And I know the sea. Aeroplanes, now, they're different. I wouldn't go anywhere near one of those things. And remember, I wasn't with Rob when it happened. Might have been better if I had.'

'How?'

'I don't think I'd have gone out. Rob probably wouldn't have either.'

'Are you sure he went out?'

Neilie looked at Iain.

'What else could he have done? If he didn't, then where is he?'

Iain grimaced.

'To tell you the truth, I was getting it into my head that it might be him in the old house.'

Neilie looked at him in animated disbelief.

'What, you think the sea threw him up there or something?'

'No, I thought maybe something else had happened, especially after you told me that you hadn't gone on the boat with him, hadn't even seen him getting into the boat.'

'You know your trouble?' said Neilie, shaking his head. 'You think too damn much. You think about things until they don't make sense any more. Always have.'

Eventually they came abreast of the automated lighthouse on the headland. A thin, iron ladder bolted to the cliff face ran down to the sea. In the days of manned lighthouses this was how the supplies were delivered. There was no need for it now. No lighthouse men now, just electronics.

From this point on a clear day you could see the notorious Flannan Isles. About a hundred years ago, three keepers had disappeared from the lighthouse there in unexplained circumstances. The table was set for their meal and, except for an overturned chair, everything was in order. But the men were gone and no trace of them was ever found. Everyone had a theory; a freak wave, a sea monster, one of them driven to murderous madness by the isolation, but the truth was never established. So near to another lighthouse, Iain was reminded of the story. Was it any wonder he was fearful of the sea?

Neilie cut the engine and the hole left by the chugging of the motor was filled by silence.

'Throw us that bag, will you?' he asked.

Iain tugged a hard canvas bag from beneath his seat. It was very heavy and he needed both hands to pull it.

'A few supplies to keep us going,' winked Neilie, thrusting his hand into the bag. Amid much clinking of tins and a bottle, he pulled out two lines. They were simple wooden frames shaped like an 'H' and wound with bright orange string. He tossed one to Iain.

Each line had a small lead weight tied around it and six or seven hooks spaced at regular intervals, each disguised by a cast of feathers. Normally this was like the fly used in fly fishing, but Neilie had taken to clipping clumps of white hair from the breast of his collie dog and using that to hide the hooks. It was a practice passed down by some older fishermen and he found it extremely effective.

'The poor dog bald again?' asked Iain with a smile.

They dropped their lines and let them drift, pulled down by the lead weights. Then it was simply a case of jigging them up and down and waiting for the fish to bite. Cod and mackerel were the most common catch, the cod from the bottom of the sea, the mackerel from nearer the surface.

With the lines in place, Neilie thrust a can of Tennent's to Iain.

'Get that down you, boy.'

As he peeled open his ring pull, Iain heard over his shoulder the unmistakable sound of the lid of a bottle being unscrewed.

'How about a chaser to go with it?'

'No thanks.'

'Well when it gets cold, you let me know if you change your mind.'

Neilie gurgled down a big mouthful of whisky and smacked his lips. The two sat in silence for a few minutes as they jerked their lines up and down, trying to attract the attention of the fish beneath. There were plenty, species of all sorts, but it was the cod and the mackerel that they would bring home.

The boat rode the swell comfortably. Neilie felt weight on his line and pulled it in with enthusiasm. Two cod, their reddish-brown scales speckled with black spots, flipped and flapped out of the water, the hooks embedded in their mouths. Neilie's spirits were up.

'There you go, my beauties. A good start.'

Grasping them by their tails, he tore them from the hooks and whapped each one against the bench of the boat. Their flailing stopped. He dropped his line back into the water again and took another swig from the bottle.

'Is the sky darkening a bit?' asked Iain.

'It's evening. It will be.'

'No, I mean the clouds are getting darker.'

Neilie glanced disinterestedly at the sky.

'Maybe.'

'Shouldn't we think about getting back?'

'You're joking! We've hardly got started. What are you so edgy about? We'll keep an eye on the weather, but we've got plenty of time. Anyway, you've still to catch something. Have another beer.'

Iain left his line in the water but he kept an anxious eye on the horizon. The clouds were getting closer every time he looked. Was the billowing of the sea getting more pronounced? They fished on in silence.

Suddenly Neilie jerked in his line again. Another cod, and one Iain didn't recognise. Then he felt a tug on his own line. He began to slowly wind it in.

'Have you got something? Good.'

The wooden frame jolted and shuddered in his hand as the hooks wound close. Then he could see the fish thrashing just below the surface. With a triumphant cry, he yanked it out of the water and into the boat. A solitary cod. He didn't have Neilie's dexterity and he couldn't grasp it. Neilie put his own line down. Jamming his cigarette between his lips, in one motion he pulled the fish from the hook and killed it.

'You can do the next one yourself. We need to get you out here more often. What are you like? Have you forgotten everything you ever learned?' Neilie teased.

'I caught a fish, didn't I? Better than I did the other night.'

'Aye, true.'

As they bantered, the boat suddenly pitched, enough almost to unbalance Iain from his seat.

'What was that?' he asked in alarm.

'Maybe we'd better get back now.'

'I told you. I bloody well told you that it was looking bad.'

'Don't panic. There's plenty of time.'

At that, the sea reared again. The wind was rising. Further down the coast, wave tops were beginning to crash against the rocks. Neilie wound in his line, threw his cigarette over the side and then took another swig of whisky. There was little left in the bottle.

'Will you stop messing about and get going,' urged Iain. 'How much of that stuff have you had?'

'Enough not to feel the sea move,' winked Neilie.

He fired the engine again and steered the boat back

round. A wave struck them broadside and sea splashed in.

'We're not going to make it back to the bay, Neilie. No chance.'

Neilie looked around him. A veil of rain was moving in swiftly and the tops of the waves were whipping up white. Neilie turned the boat again and set it ploughing towards the cliffs.

'If we can get to the lighthouse ladder we'll be fine.'

Iain's heart was thudding and as the first of the rain smacked his head, aggressive and cold, he fought down his rising panic.

'What d'you want me to do?'

Neilie's casual manner was gone. There was no disguising the seriousness of their situation.

'Bale out some water.'

Iain searched frantically for a container, eventually emptying their fish catch out of a small bucket. Concentrating on doing something helped hold the fear at bay.

The cliffs loomed, black and terrifying. Blades of rock slashed through the waves. Neilie was attempting to steer the boat towards a sheer area of cliff beneath the ladder. The ladder didn't extend all the way down to the water and Iain understood that he would have to judge his moment, delaying until the sea lifted the boat high enough for him to swing himself onto it. Neilie pulled an oar from the bottom of the boat and pushed it against the wall of rock to keep them from smashing against it.

Iain managed to grab the ladder, but at the last second his nerve failed. Had he not released his grasp, he would have been wrenched out of the boat.

'C'mon!' yelled Neilie, the aggression in his voice dulled by the hiss of the sea.

Iain was bending from his waist, his legs almost straight,

his hands holding onto the side of the boat. Up it went again, but not high enough, then it plummeted with the rebounding water. Then again, this time a little higher. Iain threw both arms at the ladder, pushed back against the boat and sprang up. His left hand caught a rung, his right slipped, tearing the skin, but he managed to thrust his knee onto another spar just as the boat fell away. Barely able to see because of the salt water stinging his eyes, Iain flung his right hand up again and this time grasped the side of the ladder. He was oblivious to the crunch of knee cap against iron as he pulled himself upright. He caught his breath and, holding on tightly, twisted round to see what he needed to do to help Neilie.

Neilie was pulling away from him, the prong of the boat splashing through the waves. Iain waved frantically. Neilie was shaking his head and shouting something, but Iain couldn't hear a word.

'Neilie!' screamed Iain. 'Neilie!'

He yelled until his throat hurt, but Neilie kept drawing away, till the noise of the engine was lost in the roar of the angry sea. Torrential rain hammered down.

'Neilie!' he yelled.

He couldn't even hear his own voice now. The peak of a huge wave lashed him, flicking his legs off the ladder. He scrambled to regain a foothold, the toes of his boots scraping frantically against the rock face. His breath came in gulps, grateful gasps of life. Another vicious arc of water was surging towards him. He burrowed his face in his arms, bracing himself. As he did so, he registered that he had seen nothing but the wave. Neilie was gone.

The wave compressed him against the rock, submerging him completely. Then he felt the wind on his head and knew he was still holding on.

The raw instinct to survive kicked in. He began to climb the ladder, rung by treacherous rung. It rattled alarmingly. Some of the bolts fastening it to the cliff wall must have been loosened by the elements. The next big wave thrashed just below his feet. He kept on climbing, climbing, drawing away from the churning, seething, pounding ocean below.

Eventually, he felt certain that he was beyond the grasp of the waves. The ladder stretched into the darkness above, the metal rasping ominously. The danger wasn't over yet. There was no guarantee that it would continue unbroken to the safety of the lighthouse. But he had no option. He couldn't go back. He held his body close against the deadly cold metal and climbed again. The thought of Neilie began to torture his mind. Where was he? The red paint used to protect the iron from erosion by the elements had mostly flaked off, and what he grasped onto was the exposed, corroded metal. His lacerated fingers stung viciously with every hand-hold.

Suddenly he could see the sweeping beam of the lighthouse above. He had nearly made it. The relief was short-lived. The next section of the ladder was bashed and twisted, one side-rail torn away completely, the rungs contorted and useless. His euphoria evaporated and panic gripped him. But in that desperate moment he found his courage. The will to live longer.

If he stood on the final rung and supported himself against the remaining side-rail, he might be able to stretch up to where the ladder continued. It was his only option. He couldn't go back down, he'd be pulped by the sea. If he tried to stay where he was, the gale would soon tear his exhausted body off the cliff.

Clutching the side-rail with both hands, he set his feet on the last safe rung. His legs trembled spasmodically as he painfully inched his hand up the rail, until he was standing at his full height. His fingertips scraped the bottom of the next fixed section. Gripping the rail, oblivious to the ragged iron cutting into his flesh, he slowly pushed his heels up until he was standing on tiptoes. The extra reach that gave him allowed him to curl the fingers of his right hand round the next rung. With a rush of adrenaline, he released his left hand from its anchor on the rail and slapped it hard above. Now he was at full stretch, spanning the broken section, his arms extended and straining in their sockets. The wind whipped him and the crystal sharpness of the rock face cut him.

If he made a mistake, if luck wasn't with him, he was dead. All those years of fearing death, and now he was faced with it, it meant nothing to him. Nothing. He willed the upper rung to hold. His foot searched for any crevice or protrusion on the rock, anything that might give him leverage. The chunky rubber of his boots was a serious impediment, but he managed to jam his foot into a small cleft. Then the other foot. The upper section held. Moving his hands up to the next rung he repeated the process until he could swing his right foot onto the bottom rung of the upper section. But when he tried to repeat the manoeuvre with his left foot, there was a jolting tug on his jacket. One of the ragged rungs from the broken section had caught on his pocket and he couldn't free himself. He had to pull himself through several contortions to shrug the jacket off. As soon as it slipped from him, the gale grabbed its trophy and twirled it into the meshing storm below. That image, more than the cold wind against his wet shirt, made him shudder.

He hauled himself over the top of the cliff and stumbled the few feet to the lighthouse, where he sat in its shelter, his chest heaving, his mind a blank. Death had been at his shoulder.

Now he faced a three-mile walk over the moor. The hill the lighthouse was built on fell away steeply and he forced himself to gather his wits and concentrate on negotiating the slithering descent. Then he faced another sharp ascent. He found his thoughts turning to Neilie.

Where was he? Had he known that the ladder wasn't safe? Was that why he hadn't followed him? With all his experience of the sea, Neilie had ignored the threat of the storm. We'll take the risk, he'd said. He had been determined that they would go out on the water. Flashes of their earlier conversations came back. Neilie knew that he hadn't alerted the police about the skeleton. Had he deliberately left him to die on the ladder? There was also the wretched possibility that Neilie might now be dead, and it would never be known for sure whether he had twice had murder in his heart.

In smothering darkness, Iain stumbled and lurched his way across bogs and streams, peat banks and ridges of rock. At last he saw the pinpricks of light from the village. He was home.

'Oh, mo ghraidh, mo ghraidh,' cried his mother as he reeled through the door. She threw her arms around his sodden frame.

'I thought you were lost.'

'I'm fine, Mam, really.'

'Your hands, look at the blood on them.' His bedraggled appearance told of his fearsome struggle to survive.

'What happened? And Neilie? Where's Neilie? Catriona is beside herself.'

She grabbed a towel from the rail on the stove and began

to rub his soaking head vigorously.

'Mam, let me get these things off first.' He unbuttoned his shirt.

'Look at the state of you. Your hands! Let me get some bandages. There's no word from Neilie. Did you see him? Was he with you?'

Iain stripped down to his underpants and began to dry himself. His crimson, bloodied hands were agony as they warmed up.

'I'll get a hot bath running. Should I get the doctor?' There was no interruption in her flow of words as she disappeared to the bathroom.

'Do you know what's happened to Neilie? I must call Catriona. She phoned me as soon as the storm hit. She was in such a state. I hope he's alright. What made you go out in that?'

Fully undressed and with a towel wrapped around his waist, Iain sank into a chair and pressed another warm towel against his face. He was trembling again. He could imagine Catriona, waiting for her husband to come home. Throughout the centuries island women had endured these long, lonely watches. But if Neilie did return, then would come the reckoning. Neilie was his oldest friend. Was he evil, or was it his own thoughts that were evil? He had to know. His mother came back into the kitchen.

'That's the bath running for you now. Catriona was calling the coastguard. I'll phone her to tell her you're home and you can tell her what happened. Did you see Neilie? Dear Lord, I hope he's safe.'

Her nervous stream was cut short by the ringing of the phone.

Chapter Fifteen

'OH MERCIFUL LORD! And he's okay? I was just about to phone you. Yes, just a moment ago. He's fine, he's fine.'

Iain listened to his mother's excited voice. Neilie was home safe. He could imagine Catriona's relief on the other end of the line, but his own heart was cold. Neilie had left him for dead, he was sure of that now.

Mary came rushing through.

'That's Catriona,' she announced unnecessarily. 'Neilie's home, safe and well. Just came through the door this minute. He was telling her to get the coastguard out for you, but I told her you were safe too. Oh, that's a scare we had. I think Neilie's wanting to speak to you.'

Iain considered for a moment.

'Tell him I'm in the bath. I'll call him later.'

'Don't you want to speak to him?'

'Just tell him I'm in the bath.'

His mother disappeared, shaking her head. As he walked through to the bathroom he could hear snippets of her conversation with Neilie over the splattering of the water. Steam was everywhere as he turned off the taps and stepped into the piping water. It should have been much too hot, but given the shivering in his bones, he savoured sliding into it. He lay back his head and felt the warmth creep through him. The cuts on his hand stung sharply.

Mary came and spoke to him through the door.

'It's alright Mam, just open it.'

She did so hesitantly. The open door shielded most of

the bath, so from the door frame she could only see his head and shoulders.

'What happened to him?' Iain asked.

'He was wanting to know what had happened to you and I couldn't tell him because I still don't know.'

'I'll tell him myself soon enough. What about him?'

'Well, he didn't say much, just that he managed to get the boat back to the river and walked home from there. Catriona told me he was soaked through. I told him you'd phone. He was so relieved to hear you were safe.'

Iain nodded doubtfully.

'Oh, I was so worried when that gale blew up. I couldn't help but think back to the night poor Rob was lost. What happened?'

Iain kept strictly the facts, without his own interpretation. Mary listened with her hand clasped to her mouth. When he described how Neilie had left him on the ladder, she said, 'The poor man probably couldn't get off the boat on his own.'

Iain resisted the urge to discharge his anger. He would save that. Later, sitting in front of the fire with a whisky warming him from the inside, the phone rang. It was Neilie again, but Iain gestured emphatically that he didn't want to talk. Mary said in an unconvincing voice that Iain had gone to his bed. He could hear Neilie asking something.

'Well I don't know. I suppose…'

Iain looked up when his mother's voice cut short.

'He's on his way up here,' she said, perplexed. 'He hung up before I could say anything else. What's happened between you two? Why don't you want to talk to him?'

Iain finished his whisky in a gulp and poured himself another. He didn't know what to do. Two minutes later, headlights flashed through the windows and a car drew

up outside. There was a knock at the door, but Neilie
swung it open without waiting for a response. Catriona
followed immediately behind. Iain stood rigidly upright.
Neilie looked at him and shook his head thankfully.

'That was close, eh?'

'Where did you get to?' accused Iain instantly.

Neilie seemed highly taken aback.

'Eh? You saw me. I was on the boat.'

'So why leave me on the ladder?'

'I didn't leave you on the ladder,' answered Neilie
defensively. 'I couldn't get onto it. '

Iain shook his head in disbelief. Neilie was riled.

'What's the matter with you? I'm telling you I couldn't
get on the ladder. The boat was kicking all over the place.
There was no way I could keep it steady. I couldn't even
stand up. I had no chance of getting on the ladder. Listen,
I thought I was a goner.'

'No, you didn't think you were a goner. What the hell
were we doing out there anyway?' shouted Iain. 'I told
you there was a storm coming. I could see it, why couldn't
you? You of all people.'

'The forecast was wrong. I didn't expect it so quick.'

Neilie was shouting back.

'It was clear enough to see. Remember the clouds. You
didn't need a forecast. That was madness going out in
that. Then you drop me off on a ladder to get smashed
against the rocks while you take off in the boat.'

'What the hell are you getting at?' yelled Neilie, taking
a step towards him.

'You know damn well what I'm getting at. You didn't
expect to see me back.'

Neilie looked stunned. The two women stood silent
and aghast.

'Don't give me the innocent look,' ranted Iain. 'You tried to do to me what you did to Rob and you know it. You tried to kill me the way you killed him.'

The accusation hung there, echoing in everyone's heads, sliding down the walls. Mary whimpered and Catriona stared at Iain. Neilie's body was taut, his face set. No one moved.

'You've lost your mind. Lost your mind.'

At that, Neilie whirled away and out the door. Catriona couldn't tear her look away from Iain.

'There was no need for that,' she almost hissed. 'What on earth possessed you to say that?'

'Because it's true.'

'What do you mean it's true? That he killed Rob? He feels bad enough already without you throwing that at him. You know what that'll do to him. You know, don't you? You, you're supposed to be his friend.'

'Yeah,' snarled Iain back, 'That's what I thought too. Didn't stop him trying to leave me to die though, did it? Ask him about the bones at the old house. Ask him who it is and how he got there. You ask him. All this crap about poor Neilie this and poor Neilie that, he feels so bad about Rob. So he should. He killed him, the murdering bastard that he is, and he tried to kill me too. You ask him about that.'

Catriona ran out of the room. Iain slugged back the shot of whisky in his glass. Mary sat down in her chair, her hands gripping her knees.

'Maybe you should stop drinking that stuff,' she said quietly. 'It makes you say such dreadful things.'

Iain grimaced as the whisky slipped down his throat.

'It's the truth that's dreadful, Mam, not my saying it. He tried to kill me tonight.'

'Neilie? You don't know what you're saying. You've had a shock. You must have, to say things like that. Go to your bed and I'll call out the doctor.'

'Don't call any doctor. It's the police we need to call.'

'Police? Now Iain, listen, you're not well. You should go to your bed.'

'I'm calling the police,' said Iain, picking up the receiver.

Mary rushed towards him and tried to pull the handset from him.

'Oh please, Iain, don't call the police,' she begged. 'Not tonight. If you want to call them in the morning then do that, but not tonight. You're not talking any sense. They'll take you away to the hospital. Please, Iain, leave it until the morning.'

Then she put her hand to her head and slumped against the arm of his father's chair.

'Mam!' He dropped the phone and grasped her arm.

'I'm okay. Just took a dizzy turn. I'm okay.'

The police forgotten, he helped her back to her chair and poured her a mouthful of whisky. She took it reluctantly and squirmed as she drank it. But then she seemed to relax a bit. The crisis had passed. He made sure she was settled and then made her a cup of tea. When he returned, she was sitting straight-backed in the chair.

'Well that was a wee turn,' she said with embarrassment.

'As long as you're fine now.' He placed the cup in her hand. 'I'm sorry if it all got too much for you.'

'We can sort it out once we've all calmed down, but there's no need for police tonight.'

'Don't worry. No police tonight.'

Mary sipped the hot tea and then looked up at her son.

'You didn't really mean any of that did you? And what was all that about bones in the house?'

'Somebody's been buried there, Mam.'

'In the old house? But how could there be?'

She was getting anxious again.

'Leave it, Mam. We'll leave it all to the morning. We'll both feel better for a night's sleep.'

The dramatic energy dispersed and a fragile calm descended. Iain helped his mother to bed.

'Promise me you'll do nothing else tonight.'

'Nothing until tomorrow, I promise. Tomorrow.'

He slept in fits and starts, never relaxed enough to drift off into a deep slumber. He was worried about his mother and he felt shattered. Dawn took a long time to drag itself over from the east.

At nine, Mary came in with some tea and toast. There was some colour back in her face.

'How are you this morning, a' ghraidh? Feeling yourself again?'

'I'm fine. The hands are a bit sore, otherwise fine.'

He phoned the Police Station when he got up. Constable Gibson's wife told him her husband had been in town overnight and she expected him home mid-morning. Iain left a message to meet him down at the old house as soon as he returned.

Iain would have spent the night there guarding the bones had his mother not taken her bad turn. If they had been removed there would be no evidence of anything. But he couldn't have left Mary alone in that state.

Mary watched him pulling on an old oilskin.

'Where are you going?' she asked.

'Just down to the house.'

'But you can't do anything with your hands like that.'

'I'm not going to be doing much.'

'Maybe you should go round and talk to Neilie first. What you said last night... You should speak to him. Sort it out with him.'

'Yes,' he smiled, 'I'll probably be doing that.'

'Good.' She was encouraged.

A strong wind blowing in from the Atlantic bullied the grass. Clouds scudded across the sky. This invigorating air would clear his head, he thought.

Evidence of the previous night's gale was everywhere. An old wooden gate had been blown over, a plastic bag flapped on a barbed-wire fence, water glimmered in the ditches. The sea was calmer, but he could hear the waves still pummelling the rocks and taste the salt in the air.

Braggan's loom was at work and a couple of children, well wrapped, were out playing. One of them waved at him as he walked by.

The aftermath of the storm was even more apparent on the shoreline. Seaweed was strewn across the stones in strands and fronds. Jellyfish, glistening dully like dying eyes, were lumped among the pebbles. A corpse, most likely a young seal, lay in a forbidding mound just above the water's edge. Plastic containers and wooden creels were scattered haphazardly.

The tent remained in place, just. Some of the lines had been snapped and it flapped urgently like a bird struggling to fly, but staked to the ground.

Iain walked through the doorway, uncertain of what he might see. Had Neilie got here before him? But nothing was out of place. The tarpaulin, protected by the walls and weighed down by the stones, was exactly as he had left it. There was nothing to do now but wait for the police to arrive. The restless unease of the past days would soon be over. He lit a cigarette and sat down, the wind whistling over the top of the wall, unable to claw at him, but snatching the smoke from his mouth and whirling it away into nothingness. He took a blast of whisky from the bottle he'd brought and looked at the hills around him.

His people had kept animals on these braes for lifetimes. There was a photograph of his great-grandfather standing just a few yards from here with his beasts grazing around him. The white Edwardian beard and the flat cap described a different era, but the landscape was the same, the sea still swept the bay, the birds cried and the smell of salt and peat tasted the air. So long ago, it seemed, but really it was no time at all.

And poor Rob, lying there, part of that past, yet connected to the present by the memories of those who had known him. He'd been dead now almost as long as he'd lived. 'I shall pass this place but once', that's what the old Quaker prayer said. How did it end? 'I shall not pass this way again.' It had been a brief passage, Rob's life, but he had left his mark and that could not be erased. It fell to those remaining to call his killer to account. Rob deserved nothing less.

What had these walls seen? What torments of mind? His great-grandmother, the nights before her sons went off to war. Calum and Finlay ahead of their emigration, knowing that they would never see this place again, nor the mother and father who had raised them. And before, others leaving because the place that reared them could no longer support them. Long nights wracked by the coughs of terminal illness. Dire famine where there was too little to fill the aching bellies of hungry children.

How many across the globe were bound to this house of stones, now open to the wind? The blood from here had been borne to Canada, the United States, to Australia,

New Zealand. Yes, and to South Africa and the Argentine, continental Europe, mainland Scotland and England. People unknown to each other, but all bearing a fragment that linked them to this wild edge of the Atlantic where the winds roamed free and strong and the grand ocean was lord of all.

Perhaps it was best to leave the house as a monument to that past. The thought had been growing on him. Neilie may have had his sinister reasons for not wanting the house resurrected, but he had been right, and so had his mother. Remember the past, respect it, learn from it, enjoy it, but to try to recreate it was folly. It couldn't be done. He understood that now. Besides, how could he make his home over the grave of his friend?

When the events of today were played out he would return to the other house, the house that had always been home, deal with the issues of the present and look to his future. The old house would outlast him; it would always be here when he needed to touch the past again.

He took another swig of the whisky and lit a second cigarette.

A stone clattered just outside. Iain tensed and lurched to his feet, throwing down his cigarette. He was no longer alone. He stepped over to the landward wall and peered over. He caught a glimpse of a crown of brown hair, but the figure ducked out of sight. Iain decided to climb onto the top of the wall and take the intruder by surprise.

Placing his hands evenly apart, he braced his arms, wincing at the pressure on his cut palms, then heaved his body onto the wall, pulling his legs up behind him. There was nobody to be seen. He edged slowly along, his breath coming in short bursts.

Suddenly there was a movement to his left and as his

head shot round Peter emerged from his tent. Both men exclaimed loudly at the unexpected appearance of the other.

'Peter! Where have you been? You gave me a fright there.' Iain sat upright.

'We do it to each other again,' laughed the German with relief.

'Where have you been? We were getting worried about you.'

'I am sorry. I have been away.'

'Where?'

If Peter was puzzled by the question, it didn't show.

'With friends. I was on a long walk,' he pointed to the south, 'and I met people I knew from when I was here before. They ask me to stay for a few days.'

'We were all worried about you. There's been helicopters looking for you.'

Peter looked shocked. Iain grinned.

'Don't worry. You've done nothing wrong, it was just me panicking. I thought you'd fallen or something like that.'

'I see. Yes, it would have been best if I had told you, but I didn't know how to contact you. I did see you here, from the cliffs, but you left before I came down. After that I went on my walk and I did not expect that I would not be back later.'

'Don't worry. Really. It's just good that everything's okay. The policeman is coming down later and I can tell him that you've been found.'

The furrow returned to Peter's forehead.

'For me?'

'No, he's coming about something else, but I can tell him.'

'I am leaving today. I came back to get my things.'

'Where are you going?'

'I'll go home and then I will go away again. It is the way I live.'

Iain watched as Peter went into the tent and packed away his belongings. When he came out, he set down his rucksack and quickly and expertly dismantled the tent. Iain saw the flask lying at the top of the open rucksack.

Peter saw him looking at it.

'Lisa. Her ashes, you know.'

Iain failed to hide his astonishment.

'I like to keep her with me,' explained Peter. 'Maybe I will leave her here some day. When I'm ready.'

'Will you be coming back?'

'Oh yes. Like I said, it is a special place.'

Peter was pulling the rucksack onto his back. He extended his hand. Iain dropped from the wall and shook it warmly.

'Safe journey.'

'Thank you. Good luck.'

Iain watched him walk to the roadside. He turned and waved and then disappeared round the bend.

Iain checked his watch. The hands were closing in on noon. Then, beneath the natural sounds around him, he heard the drone of an approaching car. He returned to the house and sat up on the wall again, waiting for the policeman to appear. It seemed to be a long time before he heard footsteps on the grit of track.

It took him a moment to register that it wasn't the constable, it was a very elderly man. The man was a stranger but there was something about his demeanour that suggested that he knew where he was going. He was dressed in a grey fedora and a charcoal, single-breasted suit beneath a dark, herringbone overcoat. He was wearing half-rimmed, tortoise shell glasses. Half way up the path he paused for breath, raised a hand to Iain and then looked over his shoulder. Behind him was coming a woman in her mid-fifties, dressed in slacks and a navy anorak. She smiled at Iain.

As the old man drew closer he finally spoke, breathless.

'Hi, fella.' The accent was American.

'Hello,' replied Iain.

'You must be Iain. I'm Calum. It's good to meet you, boy.'

Iain jumped from the wall with a thud and shook his hand. There was strength in the grip, though little flesh covering the bones. The woman reached them. Her styled hair was losing out to the wind, which also carried the scent of her perfume. Her lipsticked mouth smiled pleasantly.

'Hi, I'm Cousin Beth.'

'Hello,' said Iain, shaking her hand. 'I'm sorry. This is just such a surprise. I wasn't expecting you.'

'No. He wouldn't let me say to anyone.'

Calum had regained his breath and was looking around him.

'Time was I could run up and down here without a thought. Now listen to me trying to get my breath.'

He looked at the house.

'So, this is the old place. Don't look much like it used to.'

Then, stepping past Iain in his highly-polished shoes, he went through the doorway and into what had been the home of his youth. Iain saw him look at the tarpaulin. He removed his hat, revealing a thin rim of close-cut white hair.

'So you found him, huh?'

Iain looked at him.

'It's my brother. My brother Finlay.'

Chapter Sixteen

'I'VE CARRIED THIS with me all my days.'

They were all back in Mary's living-room. Calum was seated on the settee, his hands resting on his thighs. He'd removed his hat and coat, but kept his suit jacket on. Underneath was a waistcoat of bottle-green moleskin. The scrawn of his neck didn't fill the collar of his neat shirt, and it looked vulnerable under the tight knot of his tie.

He had wept standing at his brother's makeshift grave. Calum had seen much in his four score years and more, but now he was overwhelmed. Holding his hat by his side, he had stood there, sobbing helplessly. Beth had put her arm around him, while Iain stood by feeling bewildered and useless.

At length, the old man had regained his composure.

'I'm sorry.'

He took his daughter's hand and looked at her.

'That's my brother, Finlay. And what I must tell you is that I put him there. But you need to know why.'

'I think we should get you back indoors. You can tell us there.'

Beth looked at Iain for support and he nodded.

'Aye. We can come back down here whenever you want.'

'I guess you're right,' said Calum, swallowing hard. 'I didn't think I'd be like this. Truth be told, I didn't know how I'd be. It doesn't feel good to see him like that, what's left of him.'

As they were going up the path to the road, Constable

Gibson arrived. Iain almost stumbled.

'Everything alright?' he asked. 'I got a message to meet you here.'

'Aye, aye, everything's fine,' Iain replied, his mind working. 'It was just to tell you that that fellow came back. You know, the German hiker. I saw him here this morning.'

'Yes. I passed him coming in the road. He said he'd been staying with friends. Everything seemed to be okay.'

'Aye. I'm sorry to have dragged you out, I just thought maybe you'd want to see for yourself.'

'Have you told the coastguard yet?'

'Eh, no.' Iain was red with embarrassment.

'Well, I'd better go and do that then.' The constable looked at Calum closely. 'Is everything okay here?'

'Yes, sir,' explained Beth. 'This is my father and it's his first visit to the old country since he left. He's overcome.'

'Can I do anything to assist?'

'No, sir, thank you. We'll take him home and he'll be fine.'

'Okay. Enjoy your stay.'

'Thank you.'

Gibson left, wondering why he had been called out.

As they stepped onto the road, Calum assured them he was fine.

'I was a little upset. I'm good now.'

He turned to look at the bay, his eyes slowly scanning the view he had once known so well.

'Y'know, out there ain't changed. Not a bit. But here,' he said turning towards the village, 'There ain't nobody here now. It's silent. Never used to be. You couldn't walk up this road without seeing somebody. Look at it now. Deserted. So many of the folks have gone.'

Beth explained that her father had wanted to fly over

as soon as he'd heard of Iain's plans.

'He said he just wanted to see the old place before it changed. I wanted him to get checked by his doctor before flying and that took a couple of days to get organised. We flew overnight last night and got a plane up from Glasgow this morning.' She pronounced the city with an 's', rather than the more familiar 'z'.

They'd come over from town in a hire car, but Beth asked Iain if he would drive them back up to the house.

'I'm not too sure on these roads. I nearly had us in the ditch a coupla times,' she smiled.

Mary was waiting at the door. Beth and Calum had called in quickly earlier to let her know they'd arrived. She served them tea in her best china and Calum began his story.

'All my life I've wanted to come back and get it done right, a proper Christian burial. It's bothered me all those years that poor Finlay never had that. Not a day has gone by, but I haven't thought of him and felt sick to the pit of my stomach.'

'What happened, Daddy?' asked Beth. Clearly he had confided none of this to his daughter.

'It was the war and what it did to him. It changed him. Finlay was a great boy. He was my older brother, right?'

Mary and Iain nodded.

'He was real good to me. Some lads can't be bothered with a kid brother, but he always had time for me, taking me fishing and all that stuff. He was good with everyone. Always cheery.'

The island accent was coming through more strongly the longer he spoke.

'He was good to our mother too. If he had any money, and there wasn't much of it in those days, he'd always give her some. And he was a big help to my father with the fishing and the crofting. That's the life he wanted to live. I don't think there was a creature or a plant around here that he didn't know the name of. Knew 'em all. And the fishing, boy, he had a knack for that! He could pull fish out where nobody else could. He was a great fella.'

Calum leaned forward and took a sip from the tea on the small table beside him.

'Anyways, the war came. The Great War. The war to end all wars is what they said. Finlay was in the Naval Reserve so he's one of the first to get the call up. Sails with the Royal Navy protecting the merchant fleet. He was sunk a couple of times. One time he was a long while in the water and I remember my mother telling me that one of the boys slipped away right in front of him. Drowned. Another time he had to man a gun while one of his shipmates bled to death right next to him. He was at the Battle of Jutland, where my brother Iain was killed. The one time he did get back on leave he was very quiet. I thought it was all a big adventure and I was full of questions about the Navy. I remember him telling me to wait until they came for me, that it would happen soon enough. Told me not to go in any earlier than I needed to. We were out by Fibhig fishing from the rocks when he said that. He said to me that war was a dreadful thing.'

Mary went round with the teapot, topping up the cups. Calum took a few moments to add milk and then continued.

'I don't really know what happened to him during the rest of the war. He stopped sending letters and my mother was always scared that she'd get another telegram. She'd already got one for Iain. 'Lost at sea' it said. She'd no remains to grieve over, no grave to go to. Iain had walked out the door and that was it, nothing of him ever came back.'

He took a sip of tea and ran his tongue around his mouth.

'Are you okay, Dad?' Beth asked.

He nodded.

'Anyways, then the war finished. There was still a lot of sadness. A lot of boys who'd gone away didn't come back, but at least there would be no more killing. That's what the folks thought, anyway. When I think of the lads lost from this village alone. There was Murdo Book, big Iain Ban, Calum Morrison. There was scarce a house in the district that didn't have a connection with someone who was killed. Then the *Iolaire* hit. It's so cruel when you think of it. All these boys who'd come through the war, lost at their home port with all their families waiting for them.'

Calum dabbed at his eyes with a hankie.

'Finlay was one of the few who survived the *Iolaire*. But he saw all these lads around him dying in the sea. And they didn't all go right away, no, they clung on as long as there was strength in their bodies. But the sea and the cold, it was too much.' He shook his head. 'It was a while before the alarm was raised. I went over with my father as soon as news came through. We hitched a lift on a cart. None of us knew what to expect. That was some journey. The silence of it. We didn't know whether Finlay was alive or dead, didn't even know for sure that he was on the boat. We just knew that he was due home. When we arrived there were already lorries and carts bringing bodies back from the shore. They were all being laid out on the battery. It was a terrible sight, terrible. Folk were coming from all over the island to identify their boys. There was one cailleach, I can still see her now, stroking her fingers through her dead son's hair, as if she was trying to comb it. And the only mark on him was a tag on his toe, that was all. She sat like that for hours. I heard of one man who came to identify the son of the widow next door and it wasn't her son, it was his own. There was another man whose brother's remains were in such a state that he told his mother he hadn't even been found. There was a sailor had two dolls in his bag for the twins he'd never seen and never would see. And all the while the carts are rolling away, taking the coffins back to their home villages. They say Stornoway ran out of coffins.'

Throughout his narrative Mary would nod and sigh. Occasionally an utterance would escape, a 'yes', or 'my mother said that.'

'The whole town was like a morgue. I can't describe it.' Calum bowed his head. 'Wretched, just wretched.'

Beth took his hand and clasped it tight.

'Anyways, we found Finlay,' Calum went on. 'He was helping load a cart. He looked fine and he sounded fine, but distant. When my father told him to come home, he refused. Said he would come home when all the boys who were lost seen to. There was no persuading him. He got mighty angry and that wasn't him at all. I was sent back to tell my mother that he was safe, but Father stayed there until Finlay was ready to come home. That was a few days later. It was late evening as I recall and they came back on one of the carts. Well Finlay walks into the house and my mother, she is hugging him and crying, but Finlay never said a single word. Father said he'd been like that all the way home. It was only later, when we sat down to eat that he spoke. As soon as he was finished he left the house, went to sit on his own. You know that rock,' he gestured to Iain with his hand, 'just a ways along the cliff? Cut like a seat?'

Iain nodded.

'Well, that's where he'd sit, just watching the sea. Couldn't get him to do anything. He didn't want to go fishing, none of the stuff he'd done before.'

'He must have been suffering terribly,' said Mary quietly.

'He sure was. They've got some name for it now, but not then. You had to get on with it. You were expected to pick up where you'd left off and that's what most of 'em did. At night you could hear him moaning in his sleep. He didn't bother anyone, just kept himself to himself. But after a while he started drinking. Finlay had never been a man for the drink. But he'd go out to the bothies and get roaring drunk. He'd talk plenty then, picking fault with everything, saying he wished he'd died with his comrades. It was real upsetting for my mother, although the next day he'd be all quiet again. Then one night he had a go at me. I said something to him and he came for me, trying to hammer me with his fists. He'd have hurt me too, if he hadn't been so drunk. And y'know, it got so that I began to hate the man he'd become. This went on for three or four years, maybe more. There was a lot of trouble on the island. All these servicemen had been promised land and it wasn't happening, so they began to leave. There was chances to go to Canada and there was talk of me going. I liked the idea, I was young and wanting to make something of myself, there was nothing for me here. I went along to this meeting in the village hall where some fella from the Canadian Government was telling us about the land we could have over there. So then it got round to maybe Finlay coming with me, a fresh start and all. I don't know if I ever heard him say it, but that was the talk anyway.'

'Dad went to Canada before coming to the States,' explained Beth to Mary and Iain. They both knew this from his letters, but nodded politely.

'It all happened about a week or so before we were due to go. He'd got himself some whisky, some of the local moonshine, and he got real bad with it. I came in and he was shouting at my mother. Now, he'd never done that before. Sure, he shouted plenty, but never at her. They were the only two in the house. I tell him to shut his mouth. So he comes at me again, his fists ready and a look in his eye. I panicked.'

Calum fell silent.

'It's okay, Dad,' comforted Beth. 'You don't need to say.'

'But I do,' he said. 'I panicked. I grabbed an old iron poker that always lay by the fireplace. I swung it and I hit him once, right on the head.'

Calum's fingers brushed his forehead where his hairline once was.

'He fell straight back. Straight back, and his head cracked against the wall. It was sickening. We were both trying to get him to breathe, to stop the blood, but he was already gone. My mother sat with his head on her lap just weeping.'

The confession stilled the room. Calum hung his head again. Beth cried softly, Mary held her hand to her mouth and Iain sat in bewildered silence.

'I didn't know what to do. I'd killed my own brother. Mother sat on the floor with him for hours saying his name over and over again. I'll never forget it.'

Calum stared into the fire.

'I've gone over and over it so often.'

'It was self-defence. You can't blame yourself for that,' said Beth.

'He was my brother.'

'Why did his body end up being where it is?' asked Iain.

Calum bit on his bottom lip before he spoke, nodding his head slowly as he did so.

'We buried him where he fell. Right there in the house.'

'But why?'

'It was my mother's idea. She figured that if we gave him a proper burial, then questions would be asked and it would end up with me being arrested. "I've lost two sons already to the war," she said, "I'm not losing another." She blamed the war for what had happened to Finlay. And she'd lost Iain before that.'

'Couldn't you just have buried him in the cemetery without anyone knowing?'

'Someone would have known. You dig a grave, somebody's going to notice that.'

'What about at sea?' persisted Iain.

'She said that she'd lost Finlay when he went away to the Navy and she wasn't sending him to sea again. I don't know, maybe she wasn't thinking straight, but she was determined enough. She wanted to protect me until I'd left the country. And after that, I don't know. Maybe it got too complicated. Of course the story was that Finlay had gone to Glasgow and left for Canada from there. Hundreds of folk went, and who was going to check? What happened was, I dug up the floor, we wrapped him in a sheet and put him in the ground and covered him over again. It was right at the spot where mother sat with her chair. I guess she thought she was looking over him or something.'

'Didn't anyone else know? Did nobody miss him?' Beth was astonished.

'If Finlay had been a regular character at that time,

maybe people would, but he wasn't. Sometimes he'd disappear for days, usually to town for more booze. My father couldn't talk to him by the end and his old friends that were left had nothing to do with him. So the fact that he was gone a while didn't raise any questions. And then came the story that he'd joined me on the *Metagama*. And once you crossed the Atlantic, who was going to know what you were doing?'

'So your mother sat above him all those years? Isn't that morbid?'

'I guess she got used to it after a while. That's the real reason she would never leave the house for good.'

'I remember my mother saying that she'd asked her to come to stay with us when she was ill and she refused,' Mary remembered. 'We thought she was being stubborn, but she must have been scared of him being discovered.'

'And once the house was closed up, who was going to find out when it fell into ruins?' Iain contributed.

'It's still horrible,' Beth murmured.

'The way she saw it, she was protecting me. And she did. Nobody ever knew, until now.'

'The sad thing is that she lost you as well,' said Mary. 'She never saw you again.'

'I never thought of it like that, but I guess you're right,' reflected Calum. 'I've never been back until now. Couldn't afford to for one thing, but I always feared getting caught. And I guess I was unsure how my mother would be with me. I mean, she was there when it happened, but the fact is that I killed him. Her son. I wrote to her plenty, but she couldn't write back. I never knew what she was thinking and I could never come back to find out. That was hard.'

'I'm sure she understood. You shouldn't concern yourself about that,' said Mary, reassuringly.

'That's the thing, though. I don't know for sure.'

He turned to Iain.

'So that's it. Now you know. He's lain there all these years. It must have been a shock to find him, son. I can't imagine what you must have thought.'

'I thought too much,' said Iain. 'Far too much. And it was all wrong.'

'I guess,' said the old man, 'I guess I want to do right by him.'

Chapter Seventeen

THEY STOOD IN a small huddle. From a distance it might have seemed that the wind was forcing their heads down. Closer, though, it was clear that their heads were lowered in prayer above a grave. The Atlantic waves pounded the shore just below the cemetery wall. The wind whistled through the fencing, flapping tufts of wool torn from the backs of passing sheep. It reeled round the stones of grey granite and black marble that marked the resting places of those gone before, sweeping over the open grave and whipping granules from the top of the mound of soil lying just beyond.

They listened as the minister, speaking in the Gaelic, begged God's mercy. When he finished, the old man in the fedora and herringbone coat stepped forward, his daughter supporting his arm. He scooped up a handful of the sandy earth and scattered it over the grave in slow arcs. It spattered on the polished coffin lid.

Stepping back, he said a silent prayer at the last resting place of his brother and turned away. It was his final farewell.

Iain was next, and then others performed the same ritual. Iain went over to his great uncle, who was standing back watching, the wind tugging at his trousers.

'Ah well. That's it now. That's it,' sighed Calum.

'It's all over,' comforted Iain.

'Aye. It's where he should always have been, next to our mother and father. There's no need to hide him anymore.'

'It's what you always wanted,' said Beth.

'It was. I can rest easy now.'

They turned and began to walk slowly away from the graveside.

Calum had volunteered to go to the police himself and confess.

'What they gonna do to an old guy like me after all these years?' he asked.

Iain had been swayed by the argument, believing it would offer the simplest, most straightforward solution. He, too, couldn't imagine that the old man would be tried. Beth and Mary wouldn't hear of it.

'I won't let you do it, Dad,' Beth had told him emphatically. 'You don't know for sure that they'll let you go. They couldn't let you walk away from it if you told them.'

The four sat up much of the night considering what to do next. Calum insisted that his brother had to be buried properly, ruling out any idea of keeping the revelations to themselves. His stance spared Iain from admitting that he had already told someone else about his discovery. It was strange being involved in a conspiracy with these people he barely knew. Yet there was no doubt in his mind of the truth of Calum's story. The old man had been under no obligation to return, nor even to reveal his part in the death of his brother. It was Calum himself who decided to inform the police. It was the only way. He was prepared to take his chances.

Constable Gibson had questioned Iain carefully when he phoned requesting him to go down to the house again.

'What is it this time?' he'd asked, with no attempt to disguise his scepticism.

'A body. I think I've found a body,' explained Iain.

The disclosure had led to a flurry of official activity. A large tent was constructed to protect the site. A collection of cars filled the road and the track. Forensic officers in protective suits examined the house in minute detail. There was some tension when Calum was questioned by a detective. He stuck to the story that his brother had disappeared after his emigration. It turned out to be enough to satisfy the investigators.

'I've been covering his disappearance all my life,' he told the family later.

There was a formal exhumation of the remains and cursory inquiries. The age of the bones was confirmed and while the skull showed evidence of foul play, all the people who might have been involved were long gone. Calum's story of his own emigration checked out. He had been on the passenger list of the emigrant ship *Metagama*, so there was no suggestion of sudden flight. There had been little delay in releasing the remains for internment.

The night after Calum's revelations the phone had rung. 'It's for you,' his mother had told Iain. 'It's a woman.' It was Melanie.

'The preliminary results are back on that bone. It belonged to an adult male and it's around sixty years old. It's not the sort of thing my project would be interested in. It's really a matter for the police.'

'Thanks, Melanie. That confirms what I thought.'

'Which was…?'

Iain told her the story, blurring some of the details.

'I had to be sure.'

'Well, I'm glad that I could help. I can have the bone back to you by tomorrow if you need it.'

They met the following day and went for lunch in one of the hotels in town. They talked a lot and they laughed together. She had touched his hands, concerned about the bandages on them. She showed interest in who he was and what he told her about himself, about his plans for re-establishing a life on the island. He learned that she'd been married before as well.

'I love my work,' she told him. 'It's fascinating and especially when I'm up here. Sometimes, though, I feel as if there should be more to life. Don't get me wrong, I have a lot of friends and I enjoy seeing them. I like walking and painting. But sometimes...' she hesitated, 'sometimes I feel there should be more. Do you understand what I mean?'

He thought he did, but he was unsure. Was she just being frank or was there an invitation there? In the spirit of starting afresh, he found the nerve to ask to see her again.

'Have you got more bones to show me?' she smiled, but she agreed willingly.

When they parted, she had touched his hand again. He couldn't get her out of his head. Each time he imagined her laughing or looking at him, he felt a fillip of pleasure. This could be the beginning of something important. They had made a connection, and he would enjoy the charge of that for itself. Who knows where it might go?

Hours after the truth had been revealed to him by Calum, Iain had made that difficult walk round to Neilie and Catriona's. He hadn't even got to the door when it swung open and Neilie shouted at him to clear off.

'I don't want you here. What are you going to accuse me of now?'

Catriona had appeared at his shoulder and turned away

immediately when she saw who it was. Iain had walked right up to the door.

'Go away,' spat Neilie.

'I'm sorry. I'm really sorry. I need to explain.'

Neilie stood barring the doorway, breathing heavily, his face red. Iain caught a faint smell of alcohol.

'Look,' he said, 'I can go away now and that's that. Or you can let me tell you why I said what I did and make my peace.'

Neilie stood chewing over what he'd said.

'Look, Neilie, you said things to me, granted not as bad, but you said some nasty things and I didn't turn you away. I'm just asking for the same.'

Neilie turned back indoors in silence, but leaving the door open. Iain followed him into the kitchen. Catriona glared at him.

'I'm not here to cause trouble, Cat. I want to say I'm sorry. There's been a lot going on and I got things twisted in my mind.'

'So is it Rob in the house or not?' Neilie interrupted.

'No, it isn't Rob.'

'Thank God for that. Bad enough him dying the way he did, but if I thought I'd left him to be killed by some madman...' The thought was left unfinished.

'Who is it?' asked Catriona.

'It's an uncle of mine, well a great-uncle actually.'

'Who?'

'Finlay.'

Neilie chewed his lips as he thought.

'I've heard the name, right enough.'

The anger was slipping from his voice.

'I was so shocked when I came across the remains and Rob's body was never found and then you told me that you weren't in the boat with him and it all just began to get out of hand, and what with that in my head and then the storm and you sailing off it all came out.'

'You really thought I could do a thing like that? You've known me since we were kids.'

'I don't know if I really believed it. I thought about it. Went over and over it.'

Catriona began to fill the kettle. Her face was hidden from him and he thought she was crying. Then he realised she was trying to suppress laughter.

'What?' he asked indignantly.

'Neilie? A murderer? Have you ever heard the like?'

'Well, he doesn't mess about with those fish.'

They were all laughing by now. They grew almost hysterical, with Catriona supporting herself against the sink, Neilie bending double on the chair and Iain leaning helplessly against the door.

Reflecting on the scene later, Iain felt deeply relieved he and Neilie would remain friends. There might be lingering issues, but they were friends and they would work them out. And the same with Catriona. Her support for her husband had been the way it should be between man and wife. She had married Neilie for better or for worse and was committed to that oath. The fact was she had chosen Neilie over him. He must deal with it.

Neilie had come to Finlay's funeral and he, Iain, Calum and Beth drove back from the cemetery to Mary's house. She had stayed at home, as was the traditional way with island funerals. Catriona had remained with her.

A lunch was ready waiting for them.

'It was very fitting,' Calum told Mary. 'Nice and simple.'

They ate and they talked. The photographs came out,

and the letters. They absorbed everything the old man said as he pointed out family and put names to anonymous faces, giving them a place they'd never had before, fleshing them out with life. The young man with the stern face and the flat cap turned out to have had great wit and humour. The lad in the dungarees went on to be one of the outstanding intellects of his generation, rising to a position of great prominence in a land far from the crofts that reared him. There was the suggestion of a first love when, peering through his bifocals, Calum spotted a girl among a group of fisherfolk.

'There's Katie! My, but she was a bonny girl, Katie. They said she was one of the bonniest girls to have come from the district.'

'Sounds like you had an eye for her?' teased Beth.

'Your mom was the only one for me. But sure, Katie was a sweet girl.'

He lingered over each photograph.

'So many of them are soldiers,' observed Beth.

'And so many of them never came home,' replied her father. 'This one, Calum Morrison, he wrote songs, that lad.' The old man started singing. His voice was high and reedy, but the words came confidently, unforgotten from the years of repetition at ceilidhs and evenings of reminiscence at home.

'See that fellow there, the one with the light hair,' he gestured at another. 'Iain Ban. Strong as an ox. I always thought he was so strong that no bullet could kill him. And it was the gas that got him in the end. This one here, Murdo Book they called him. There was talk of him going to the university, but he didn't come back from the war either.'

Another photo caught his eye, a young man in Naval

uniform and three girls in white blouses and ankle-length skirts.

'That's your mother there, Mary, my sister. There was many a lad after her, I can tell you. And that's my brother Iain with them. He was back on leave then. That wasn't long before he drowned.'

Later he read though all the letters, mouthing the words to himself. As he did so, Iain realised what it was about them that had troubled him. In Calum's own letters from across the Atlantic, there had been no mention of Finlay, no reference at all. There was no mention because both Calum and his mother knew exactly where Finlay was and why.

After dinner Calum asked Iain if they could go back to the old house.

'I'd like to take a last look at the old place before we go back.'

The sun was still bright. Even the glare on the sea was too much for the naked eye. Evening was closing in. The two men stood by the seaward wall of the house as the sky blazed through the spectrum of oranges, golds and reds.

The sea was calm. Gentle waves played against the rocks at the mouth of the bay, splashing light spray into the air. The lapping tide gurgled on the shore, with the occasional clatter of a stone being dragged back over its brothers. Beyond there was the distant breath of the ocean. The surface moved constantly, but not uniformly, with schools of small waves moving in one direction and others drifting contrarily, while draughts of wind pulled bands of water out to sea in a regular, rhythmic pattern.

Seagulls swirled down from their cliff-top nests, banking so that their wing tips almost, but never quite, caught the water, before swooping back up with yelping cries. From inland there came the song of a blackbird and the throaty rattle of sheep. Iain watched a sparrow land on the back of a grazing ewe and perch there boldly, before another arrived and the first flew off as if it was some sort of game. A family of rabbits played fifty yards away, bobbing through the rocks and their turf crusts.

The sun's aura burned golden above it just before the orb itself sank below the horizon, cupping the heavens in thanks for another day of glory. Such were the certainties here, where the sun rose and fell, the winds blew and the sea was ever restless.

As dusk shuffled its shadows over the sea and the land, the old man spoke.

'I used to know every bit of this bay, land and sea. Probably still do. I remember seeing whales out there, just out a ways. One of them washed up here, in fact. Not much of it was left after we got to it, right enough. The skin and the oil and stuff, you could make use of all of that. When I was a boy there still used to be sailing ships, you'd see them on the horizon. That was always a thrill. One ran onto the rocks there at the gully after the crew abandoned ship. That got stripped down too, pretty quick. Us kids fished off one of the old planks for years.'

His eyes were alive with memories.

They followed the path to the old house.

'Would you want to stay here again?' asked Iain.

Calum thought for a moment.

'No,' he answered definitely. 'There's nobody here. Everyone I knew is gone. I got my own family, my kids, my grand-kids and they're all back in the States. No, son, it was a fine place to grow up but I left because there was nothing for me then, and there ain't nothing for me now. Home is where your family is, where your friends are. And that's where I want to be. People have been living hereabouts since Christ and before and we don't know nothing about most of 'em. We're just passing through and we'll all be forgotten soon enough. This place has forgotten me already. It's good to know who you are, where you're from, but you can't let it tie you down. Live for those around you and you'll do okay.'

Iain listened intently. Calum's words struck a deep chord.

The two men, generations apart but of the same blood, stood quietly in front of the ruined house. A rush of wind blew in off the ocean and swept on past them as if they weren't there.

Glossary of Gaelic terms used in *Heartland*

a' bhalaich	boy
cailleach	old woman
a' ghraidh	dear
mo ghraidh	my dear
Leodhsadh	Lewisman
uisge beatha	whisky
seanacharrach	old-fashioned

Call na h-Iolaire by Tormod Calum Domhnallach (Acair, 1978) and *Metagama* by Jim Wilkie (Birlinn, 2001) will tell you all you need to know about the stories surrounding both vessels.

Some other books published by **Luath Press**

The Road Dance
John MacKay
1 842820 40 0 PB £6.99

Why would a young woman, dreaming of a new life in America, sacrifice all and commit an act so terrible that she severs all hope of happiness again?

Life in the Scottish Hebrides can be harsh – 'The Edge of the World' some call it. For the beautiful Kirsty MacLeod, her love of Murdo and their dream of America promise an escape from the scrape of the land, the repression of the church and the inevitability of the path their lives would take. But the Great War looms and Murdo is conscripted. The village holds a grand Road Dance to send their young men off to battle. As the dancers swirl and sup, the wheels of tragedy are set in motion.

[MacKay] has captured time, place and atmosphere superbly... a very good debut. MEG HENDERSON

Powerful, shocking, heartbreaking... DAILY MAIL

With a gripping plot that subtly twists and turns, vivid characterisation and a real sense of time and tradition, this is an absorbing, powerful first novel. The impression it made on me will remain for some time.
THE SCOTS MAGAZINE

Deadly Code
Lin Anderson
1 905222 03 3 PB £9.99

The past meets the future with deadly consequences

A decomposing foot is caught in a fishing net off the west coast of Scotland and forensic expert Dr Rhona MacLeod is called in on a case that takes her back to her Gaelic roots. But when the Ministry of Defence tries to shut down the story, Rhona refuses to be deflected from her quest for the truth.

The third in the Dr Rhona MacLeod forensic scientist series.

Lewis and Harris
Francis Thompson
0 946487 77 4 PB £5.99

The fierce Norsemen, intrepid missionaries and mighty Scottish clans – all have left a visible mark on the landscape of Lewis and Harris.

This guide explores sites of interest, from pre-history through to the present day.

The Glasgow Dragon

Des Dillon

1 84282 056 7 PB £9.99

*What do I want?
Let me see now.
I want to destroy
you spiritually,
emotionally and
mentally before
I destroy you
physically.*

When Christie Devlin goes into business with a triad to take control of the Glasgow drug market, little does he know that his downfall and the destruction of his family is being plotted. As Devlin struggles with his own demons, the real fight is just beginning.

There are some things you should never forgive yourself for.

Will he unlock the memories of the past in time to understand what is happening? Will he be able to save his daughter from the danger he has put her in? Nothing is as simple as good and evil.

Des Dillon is a master storyteller and this is a world he knows well.

The authenticity, brutality, humour and most of all the humanity of the characters and the reality of the world they inhabit in Des Dillon's stories are never in question.
LESLEY BENZIE

It has been known for years that Des Dillon writes some of Scotland's most vibrant prose.
ALAN BISSETT

The Blue Moon Book

Anne MacLeod

1 84282 061 3 PB £9.99

*Love can leave
you breathless,
lost for words.*

Jess Kavanagh knows. Doesn't know. Nearly twenty-four hours after meeting and falling for archaeologist and Pictish expert Michael Hurt she suffers a horrific accident that leaves her with aphasia and amnesia. No words. No memory of love.

Michael travels south, unknowing. It is her estranged partner sports journalist Dan MacKie who is at the bedside when Jess finally regains consciousness. Dan, forced to review their shared past, is disconcerted by Jess's fear of him, by her loss of memory, loss of words.

Will their relationship survive this test? Should it survive? Will Michael find Jess again? In this absorbing contemporary novel, Anne MacLeod interweaves themes of language, love and loss in patterns as intricate, as haunting as the Pictish Stones.

As a challenge to romantic fiction, the novel is a success; and as far as men and women's failure to communicate is concerned, it hits the mark.
SCOTLAND ON SUNDAY

High on drama and pathos, woven through with fine detail.
THE HERALD

FICTION

The Burying Beetle
Ann Kelley
ISBN 1905222084 PB £6.99
ISBN 1842820990 PB £9.99

Berlusconi Bonus
Allan Cameron
ISBN 1905222076 PB £9.99

Selected Stories
Dilys Rose
ISBN 1 84282 077 X PB £7.99

Lord of Illusions
Dilys Rose
ISBN 1 84282 076 1 PB £7.99

Torch
Lin Anderson
ISBN 1 84282 042 7 PB £9.99

Driftnet
Lin Anderson
ISBN 1 84282 034 6 PB £9.99

The Fundamentals of New Caledonia
David Nicol
ISBN 1 84282 93 6 HB £16.99

Milk Treading
Nick Smith
ISBN 1 84282 037 0 PB £6.99

The Kitty Killer Cult
Nick Smith
ISBN 1 84282 039 7 PB £9.99

The Strange Case of RL Stevenson
Richard Woodhead
ISBN 0 946487 86 3 HB £16.99

But n Ben A-Go-Go
Matthew Fitt
ISBN 1 905222 04 1 PBK £7.99

The Bannockburn Years
William Scott
ISBN 0 946487 34 0 PB £7.95

Outlandish Affairs: An Anthology of Amorous Encounters
Edited and introduced by Evan Rosenthal and Amanda Robinson
ISBN 1 84282 055 9 PB £9.99

Six Black Candles
Des Dillon
ISBN 1 84282 053 2 PB £6.99

Me and Ma Gal
Des Dillon
ISBN 1 84282 054 0 PB £5.99

The Tar Factory
Alan Kelly
ISBN 1 84282 050 8 PB £9.99

The Underground City
Jules Verne
ISBN 1 84282 080 X PB £7.99

POETRY

Burning Whins
Liz Niven
ISBN 1 84282 074 5 PB £8.99

Drink the Green Fairy
Brian Whittingham
ISBN 1 84282 020 6 PB £8.99

The Ruba'iyat of Omar Khayyam, in Scots
Rab Wilson
ISBN 1 84282 046 X PB £8.99

Tartan & Turban
Bashabi Fraser
ISBN 1 84282 044 3 PB £8.99

Talking with Tongues
Brian D. Finch
ISBN 1 84282 006 0 PB £8.99

Kate o Shanter's Tale and other poems [book]
Matthew Fitt
ISBN 1 84282 028 1 PB £6.99

Kate o Shanter's Tale and other poems [audio CD]
Matthew Fitt
ISBN 1 84282 043 5 PB £9.99

Bad Ass Raindrop
Kokumo Rocks
ISBN 1 84282 018 4 PB £6.99

Madame Fifi's Farewell and other poems
Gerry Cambridge
ISBN 1 84282 005 2 PB £8.99

Poems to be Read Aloud
introduced by Tom Atkinson
ISBN 0 946487 00 6 PB £5.00

Scots Poems to be Read Aloud
introduced by Stuart McHardy
ISBN 0 946487 81 2 PB £5.00

Picking Brambles
Des Dillon
ISBN 1 84282 021 4 PB £6.99

Sex, Death & Football
Alistair Findlay
ISBN 1 84282 022 2 PB £6.99

The Luath Burns Companion
John Cairney
ISBN 1 84282 000 1 PB £10.00

Immortal Memories: A Compilation of Toasts to the Memory of Burns as delivered at Burns Suppers, 1801–2001
John Cairney
ISBN 1 84282 009 5 HB £20.00

The Whisky Muse: Scotch whisky in poem & song
Robin Laing
ISBN 1 84282 041 9 PB £7.99

A Long Stride Shortens the Road
Donald Smith
ISBN 1 84282 073 7 PB £8.99

Into the Blue Wavelengths
Roderick Watson
ISBN 1 84282 075 3 PB £8.99

The Souls of the Dead are Taking the Best Seats: 50 World Poets on War
Compiled by Angus Calder and Beth Junor
ISBN 1 84282 032 X PB £7.99

Sun Behind the Castle
Angus Calder
ISBN 1 84282 078 8 PB £8.99

Details of these and other Luath Press titles are to be found at
www.luath.co.uk

Luath Press Limited

committed to publishing well written books worth reading

LUATH PRESS takes its name from Robert Burns, whose little collie Luath (*Gael.*, swift or nimble) tripped up Jean Armour at a wedding and gave him the chance to speak to the woman who was to be his wife and the abiding love of his life. Burns called one of *The Twa Dogs* Luath after Cuchullin's hunting dog in *Ossian's Fingal*. Luath Press was established in 1981 in the heart of Burns country, and is now based a few steps up the road from Burns' first lodgings on Edinburgh's Royal Mile. Luath offers you distinctive writing with a hint of unexpected pleasures.

Most bookshops in the UK, the US, Canada, Australia, New Zealand and parts of Europe, either carry our books in stock or can order them for you. To order direct from us, please send a £sterling cheque, postal order, international money order or your credit card details (number, address of cardholder and expiry date) to us at the address below. Please add post and packing as follows: UK – £1.00 per delivery address; overseas surface mail – £2.50 per delivery address; overseas airmail – £3.50 for the first book to each delivery address, plus £1.00 for each additional book by airmail to the same address. If your order is a gift, we will happily enclose your card or message at no extra charge.

Luath Press Limited
543/2 Castlehill
The Royal Mile
Edinburgh EH1 2ND
Scotland
Telephone: 0131 225 4326 (24 hours)
Fax: 0131 225 4324
email: gavin.macdougall@luath. co.uk
Website: www. luath.co.uk